The Last Santa

By

S.H. Langford

First Printing: 2016
ISBN 9781522063544

Stephen H. Langford
5876 Free State Road
Marshall, VA 20115

For Additional Ordering Information Contact us at:
TheRealLastSanta@gmail.com

Acknowledgements

I would like to thank my wife Lori who provided much needed support and encouragement. I also want to thank my mother Ann Marie Langford, brother Andy Langford, friend Mitchie Shaw and sister-in-law Robin Langford for their editorial guidance and advice.

Contents

Acknowledgements vii

1. Popping the Question 1

2. Looking for Answers 4

3. Off to Work 7

4. Expert Opinion 10

5. Decision (sort of) 15

6. Elfish Mistakes 18

7. A Short Walk 21

8. You Be the Judge 24

9. Who Are You? 27

10. What's Wrong with Them? 35

11. The Mrs. 38

12. Movement 41

13. Introductions 46

14. Circles 49

15. Lots of Questions 52

16. Caught Hiding 57

17. A Little Help 59

18. Deep Insight 63

19. Take a Ride 66

20. What's That? 70

21. Disappointment 74

22. All Alone 77

23. Curious 81

24. New Friends 83

25. Without a Trace 87

26. Who Is This? 89

27. Wandering 92

28. Getting Tired 95

29. The List 97

30. Leftovers 101

31. Glimmer of Hope 106

32. The Plan 109

33. Who's there? 111

34. Are You Nuts? 115

35. Running Out of Time 118

36. Check It Out 119

37. Empty Nest 124

38. Too Late 125

39. Now What? 132

40. Who Is That? 135

41. Then What? 137

1. Popping the Question

"… and to all a good night!"

Nani gently closed the classic book of elfin history fully expecting Jojo to be sound asleep. Instead Jojo was staring intently at the back cover of the book. It pictured Santa Claus flying off into a moon-lit night in a sleigh pulled by tiny reindeer. Santa was looking back over his shoulder waving to a little child who was looking out a window. Nani stood up and adjusted the covers around Jojo's shoulders to make sure she was comfortable. The bed had no pillow or cushion of any sort. A simple slab of solid white stone that was preferred by elves. Elves often said to each other, "Hard work deserves a hard bed." Jojo couldn't have agreed more. Her room resembled a cave. Simple, barren, and pristine. Light emanated softly from the walls. All the colors of the rainbow would gently appear and disappear, moving to different areas of the room in an infinite variety of patterns resembling the Northern lights. Soothing for a little elf at bed time. Jojo, however, was not sleepy. On the contrary, she had a confused look on her face. She looked up at Nani and very innocently asked, "Are humans real?"

Nani's pointed left ear twitched slightly. Nani was a Monitor Elf, responsible for the care and training of New Elves such as Jojo. Monitor elves are each assigned a Warren of thirteen new elves for which they are responsible from the time they emerge from their icicles until their elf 'Change'. Elfin lore views the number thirteen as magical referencing it in many different ways but from a practical perspective thirteen new elves seemed to be the most manageable number for their monitors. As new elves go through the Change, they are given permanent work assignments, removed from the warren and replaced by other new elves.

"Why do you ask that?" Nani replied, keeping her ears as still as possible to avoid revealing the tingle that ran up her spine.

Jojo stared at the book's picture, thinking about the children on the naughty list who did not receive presents. "It doesn't make sense. I mean, why aren't all children nice? Elves, fairies and gnomes aren't like that. They aren't naughty. Trolls are perhaps, but humans aren't trolls. Why would humans be naughty?"

"They are just different. We're all different."

Jojo's forehead scrunched up. "And Santa needs a list to keep track of them because there are so many naughty ones?"

Nani nodded her head causing her ears to wobble.

"Don't they want to get presents?"

"I'm sure they do." Nani paused then added, "But remember, although humans can be mean and greedy, they can also be nice and generous."

"What is 'mean and greedy'?"

"When they hurt each other and don't share."

"And that's naughty?"

"Yes."

The idea of being 'mean and greedy' to another elf was inconceivable to Jojo. After a few seconds her eyes quickly brightened. "But humans aren't real ... are they?"

"Of course they're real." Nani replied firmly, her ears straightening assuredly.

Jojo thought about this for a few more seconds. "But if they would just be nice they'd be happier, have more friends, and get presents. It doesn't make sense." She paused again, the wheels spinning rapidly in her head, "Has anyone ever seen one?"

Nani's left ear twitched again. An interesting thing about elves' ears is that they seem to have a personality of their own similar to a cat's tail. They act independently of their host (the elf's head in this case) while also revealing the host's true emotions. An elf's ears are also a good indicator of what's coming next. "Have you been talking to Schnug again? You know how gnomes exaggerate." Jojo shrugged and looked back at the picture of Santa waving. Nani added, "Besides, we spend all year making presents just for Christmas. What do you think Santa does with them?"

Without looking up Jojo replied, "Schnug says Santa takes them to the South Pole where he trades them for candy."

Nani smiled at Jojo. "Everyone knows candy comes from pixies. They harvest the sugar from the Arctic lights. It's separated by color, and then flavored and formed into candy canes, marshmallows, chocola..."

"But Nani, have you ever seen a human?"

Nani hesitated, "Well, no...but I'm sure there are many elves that have. Santa Claus, for example, sees them every year." She smiled at Jojo. "Now go to sleep. Christmas is almost here. You'll need your rest for work tomorrow."

Jojo blushed. "I know. Sometimes my mind just wanders."

Nani gently stroked the rim of Jojo's ear. Her own ears, however, began to tingle. "Get to sleep. Morning is only an hour away."

Jojo smiled back, closed her eyes and immediately fell into a deep sleep. Nani watched her for a moment then left the little elf's chamber shutting the door behind her. Nani replayed Jojo's statement, "Sometimes my mind just wanders," ... that's not normal.

2. Looking for Answers

After leaving Jojo's room, Nani walked down a brightly lit tunnel. She hoped she was overreacting but knew from past experience that minor events have a way of getting out of control if not immediately addressed. She would not be caught off guard again. She hustled through the Traditional Games facility walking by the assembly rooms for Wooden Trains, Rocking Horses and Music Boxes. She exited the tunnel and entered a large central cave. There was a buzz of activity with creatures of all sorts hustling past each other with great purpose. Everyone was polite but wasted no time as they carried packages or pushed carts full of boxes into and out of myriad tunnel entrances that led to other areas within the vast North Pole complex.

Above each tunnel was a sign indicating its destination such as Dolls, Boats, and Art. As she walked her eyes scanned for one particular unmarked tunnel that led to only one room.

This was her least desirable destination, even more so than the Electronic Games tunnel whose blaring noises, whistles, and beeps made her ears quiver and ache. She headed for the entrance just to the left of the Balls tunnel. She anxiously glanced around to see if anyone was looking then quickly entered the mouth of the tunnel and began walking briskly. The tunnel was like all the others except at the end hung a large wooden door inscribed with the odd title, Interspecies Relations. When she finally stood in front of the door she paused for a moment. The wood grain was dark from century's worth of care. She took a deep breath then turned its heavy metal handle. Despite its weight the door swung open easily with only a slight creak. The room was empty except for a book shelf and a thick leather bound book laying open on a large simple desk. An ancient elf sat at the desk. His posture was perfect with his hands resting on top of the book prepared for visitors. He appeared to be dozing. His head was tilted forward, chin resting on his chest. He didn't often have company, which was just fine with him, but he was always ready for anything, or so he thought. Nani had not been in this room for one hundred and sixty-two years. She shut the door a little harder than necessary to get his attention. His head snapped up.

He cleared his throat and with a friendly smile said, "Ah, Nani! How have you been? I haven't seen you since... the Rudolf incident... I believe." Tibit knew exactly when he had seen Nani last but did not want to make too strong a reference to that unfortunate event.

The 'Rudolf Incident' as it is unofficially known had such a reputation that, to this day, when something bad happens, an elf might exclaim, "Oh Rudolf!" in frustration. Or if a problem became worse it would be described as being Rudolfed. Over time, an acronym was created for Rudolfed (Related and Uncontrolled Development Of Little Fixes Executed Disastrously). Needless to say Rudolf the reindeer did not think much of this use of his name. Everyone realized it was not Rudolf's fault. Rudolf was, in fact, a celebrity of sorts owing to his unique gifts and strong will to succeed. Even so, no reindeer had been named Rudolf since the incident.

Tibit's smile quivered a little as he recalled that particular memory, his emotions still a bit frazzled. Nani had her own memory thinking to herself that reindeer were another species like humans who could be mean to each other. Why can't reindeer just behave and not play all those silly games? There were plenty of mistakes during the Rudolf incident, but since Nani's role at the time was to watch over the reindeer she would forever bear the primary burden for the uproar.

Tibit fidgeted in his chair. "What brings you here today?" he asked innocently, trying to be as nonchalant as his ears would allow. Since no one came to his office for social visits he offered, "No more problems with the reindeer, I hope?" He smiled weakly at his poor attempt at humor.

Nani did not return his smile. "No, Tibit. Not a reindeer issue this time. This is purely an elf matter."

3. Off to Work

Exactly one hour later Jojo's eyes popped open. She was fully rested and the earlier conversation seemed distant. Of course, humans were real. Why would anyone make that up? No one lies ...except trolls, of course, or gnomes who stretched the truth too far, but not elves for whom it is physically impossible. Lies simply can't pass their lips in the same way ears can't see one another. But, had anyone ever actually seen a human? Nani hadn't, and she was over three hundred years old. Nor did Nani know another elf that had seen one. Jojo supposed Nani was right in that Santa would have had to see many of them. She smiled to herself because if you couldn't trust Santa, who could you trust?

All the time Jojo was thinking these thoughts she was preparing for work. 'Work,' though, isn't exactly the right word for what elves do. New born elves first emerge from melting icicles in the spring. They immediately begin to organize and stack things. It is not something they choose to do or not to do, but something they have to do, like breathing or eating. Without work they would wither and die just as a plant without water. It's what they are literally born to do.

'Focus!' Jojo told herself. Her mind was wandering again, and she had at least another one hundred and thirty-four dolls to complete by breakfast with all the arms on the correct sides and the heads screwed on straight. Yet her mind continued to wander. Could this be the elf change when a new elf turns into a mid-elf? It happens to most elves between the ages of fifty-five and sixty-three. But at sixty-four it had still not happened to Jojo and she was beginning to wonder if it ever would. Jojo was not comforted much by Nani's reassurance that it would happen soon with her ears growing longer, nose hair needing regular trimming, and feet becoming more pointed (how else would they fit into those shoes?) Jojo was anxious about the Change but all the other elves had it survived over the millennia.

Jojo made her way to the to the doll assembly room. Very organized and brightly lit by a rainbow that extended diagonally from one corner of the room to the opposite corner. As you might expect a pot of gold sat under each end of the rainbow, and closely guarded by small leprechauns dressed in green suits, black top hats, chin beards, and gnarled wooden staffs. The room began to swell with activity as other elves entered. No one was in charge. Everyone had a specific job and knew where they were needed and what was to be done. If sections fell behind, additional elves appeared out of the mass of activity to help out and then blended back into the crowd after things were back on track. No one asked or directed others to help. It just happened due to a common understanding of order.

Delivery elves busily stockpiled doll parts at the various stations around the room. Jojo and the other body elves took their positions beside the bins of arms, heads and legs. Across the room the clothes elves dressed the dolls. The feature' elves took up their positions beside the hair and paint that would decorate the heads. Jojo looked at the partially assembled doll she held. Is this is really what humans looked like: pink, brown or yellow, with chubby feet, short ears and a round nose? They weren't very attractive Jojo thought, nothing like the lean, pointed features of elves with skin that shimmered like satin. She had been told these dolls looked like new humans who would very quickly grow into mid and elder humans. After only fifteen or twenty years they would become much taller, and most would remain chubby their whole lives. They grew this fast because they only lived seventy or eighty years, a hundred years at most. That's hardly enough time for an elf to earn her Apprentice Assembler certificate. Jojo received her certificate in only fifty-two years (three years early, thank-you very much). What could humans possibly accomplish in only seventy years? Even if they could be mean she felt sorry for them. They all deserved presents if for no other reason than their extremely short lives.

4. Expert Opinion

Tibit sat up a little straighter and looked intently at Nani. An issue that was purely elf related was rare indeed. Tibit was usually called upon to handle disagreements between species, thus the need for an Interspecies Relations Office. Elf only conflicts on the other hand were extremely rare. Elves had always worked well together with a collective consciousness similar to ants. If a problem occurred, order was restored and things returned to normal. An offender, if one existed, understood the mistake, learned from it and moved on. Inevitably there were too many elves offering too many solutions creating confusion. For example, should the left rear wheel be installed on the toy truck before the right front wheel? Of course problems always seemed to arise when elves interacted with trolls or fairies (and who could blame them), but a purely elf issue was unusual. A natural problem solver, Tibit thought this might be interesting.

"What precisely is the issue?" He asked with great confidence.

Nani replied, "An elf under my charge has been asking odd questions."

Tibit's right ear leaned forward slightly. This type of thing was always handled by the monitor elves like Nani. Despite their outwardly calm and congenial demeanor, elves have little patience with impractical and inefficient behavior. If any other monitor elf had brought this issue to his office he would have quickly, but politely, reminded them of their responsibilities while firmly escorting them out of his office, but he felt some sympathy for Nani since the Rudolf Incident, so he decided to indulge her, for the moment.

He asked in as pleasant a tone as he could muster, but noticeably impatient, "Odd questions such as...?"

Nani hesitated, measuring her response. The implications for Jojo could be serious. As much as she wanted to protect the little elf, this could not be ignored and would not go unnoticed for long. Nani knew all too well the consequences of letting issues grow out of control. With a little luck it would all be attributed to the elf change, and things would quickly go back to normal. She took a breath then replied, "One of my new elves asked me if humans are real."

Tibit's eyes widened. Now his left ear leaned forward and turned slightly in the direction of the right ear as if to confirm what it just heard. "That is an odd question for a new elf... well... any elf, for that matter." Tibit paused and mindlessly fondled the tip of his ear. "'Are humans real?'" he repeated to himself out loud, "...unheard of..." His opposite ear seemed to wiggle in agreement.

He looked back into Nani's eyes, "Has she gotten the proper minutes of sleep each night?"

"Absolutely!" Nani was very sensitive to any questions about her attentiveness to her warren. "She gets no less than fifty-six minutes and no more than sixty-seven minutes of sleep a night."

Tibit opened his mouth to offer another suggestion but Nani continued, cutting Tibit off, "And, yes, she drinks plenty of hot chocolate with the appropriate number of marshmallows before bed."

Tibit held up his hands in defense. "I'm sorry, I just needed to ask. This could be a serious matter, and I need to cover the basics." He hopped off the stool he was sitting on and made his way around the ancient desk. Speaking out loud again, more to himself than to Nani, "This could just be a case of the elf change, you know."

Nani thought, 'He's telling me that?! As if that weren't the first thing I considered!' However, her expression remained void of any emotion.

Tibit crossed the little room to shelves that held a series of books with titles such as _The Unpredictable Troll_, _Gnomes: Get to Gnow Them_ and _Fairies as Friends_. He grabbed a book titled _The Unexpected Elf_. Besides being very dusty, it appeared to be un-used. Tibit examined the index, "You know most of the questions asked of this office are regarding gnomes. They are very strange creatures. Did you know they are allergic to yellow candy? I once had an emergency call from a gnome complaining their young tu-ber was tricked into eating a lemon drop. Tricked by an elf... unheard of. When I tried to explain that..." He noticed Nani's ears vibrating slightly. "Yes, of course, but that is not relevant to the issue at hand is it?" He carried the elf book back to the desk and climbed onto the stool. "Did you consider increasing the work load? Sometimes that helps new elves get back on track."

"Jojo is unable to keep up as it is," Nani replied.

"I see... Any issues with other elves? You know, not helping out, not speaking, slow to apologize?"

Nani shook her head, "No."

Tibit's eyes narrowed slightly, "Have you tried..." Nani's ears began to vibrate again. He paused, "Yes, yes, of course you did."

Tibit looked back at his book apparently stumped. "Have there been any other strange things going on?"

Nani paused for a moment, "Jojo is frequently... distracted."

Tibit looked up from the book, "Distracted? Distracted how?"

"She says her mind 'wanders'. I'm not really sure what that means but it sounds serious."

Tibit finished scanning the index for the word, or some deriv-ative of 'distraction.' Finding none, he closed the cover, scratched his ear, and went back to the book shelf and grabbed another, very large book. The title made Nani's heart skip a beat: _Humans Explained_.

"Why are you looking at that?" Nani asked.

Tibit wiggled back to the top of the stool. "The elf reference books generally proscribe how many twists of licorice must be consumed to ease melancholia, identify the optimum working age, and how to cure an excessive sense of euphoria. But this kind of distraction is uncommon." Tibit thought 'That is an understatement! Honestly it sounds more human-like than elfish.'

Nani hesitated, and then offered, "Well, she did get the initial thought from a gnome. Who knows what rattles around in those heads?"

Tibit's ears wobbled in agreement. "I knew a gnome once who played a trick on a fairy where he grabbed her wings while she was asleep and..."

Nani glared at Tibit.

Tibit coughed lightly, "Yes, yes, but planting the seed requires fertile ground upon which the seed can grow." Nani reluctantly agreed. Tibit continued, "My concern is what fertile ground is rattling around in Jojo's head?"

Tibit scanned the _Humans Explained_ index for Wandering Minds. Nothing. He found a reference to a Waggery (mischievous play), Wanderlust (a desire to explore), and Wanton (a spoiled child)—all appropriate descriptions for humans but none that fit this particular circumstance. He did find a section on Distraction, but it only described the symptoms, not the cure. In fact, it did suggest it was incurable, but he did not want to tell that to Nani. Not yet anyway. The last thing he needed was a distracted monitor elf! The irony of a distracted monitor elf made Tibit smile. His ears tingled in agreement.

Nani leaned forward. "What is it? Did you find something?"

Tibit adjusted himself on the stool and replied, "Not directly. Something for future investigation perhaps." He continued to browse the thick book. Finally he stopped, exhaled deeply, closed the book and announced sadly. "There is only one thing left to do."

5. Decision (sort of)

Nani's eyes grew very large. Both ears shivered in unison and seemed to shrink ever so slightly. She understood that Jojo needed help, and for the safety of the other elves, Jojo would likely have to be separated so she wouldn't infect the others with her ideas. But she knew from the Rudolf incident that Tibit was strictly by the book. This could only mean banishment. Banishment was rare but the ultimate solution for the most difficult of problems. Jojo would immediately be isolated from the others and ushered away from the North Pole. The sense of shock, fear and emptiness all collided in Nani at the same time. "Are you sure that is really necessary? She is only sixty-four years old after all."

"Sixty-four is young I grant you, but given the circumstances...." Tibit's eyes squinted in confusion. His ears tilted in agreement. "It seems to be the most obvious choice. I don't understand. Is this a problem for you?"

"'A problem for me?'" Nani blurted out as she became agitated. "She's part of my warren. I'm very concerned for her well-being. How should I feel?"

"Perhaps relieved or even pleased."

"Relieved!? Pleased!?" Her voice began to rise. "She is only a new elf. Why should I be 'relieved,' much less 'pleased'?"

Tibit hesitated and added reassuringly. "It's not that bad."

"How can banishment not be 'that bad'!?"

Tibit hesitated again, his ears stood perfectly still. "Banishment?! Who said anything about banishment?"

"You did."

"I never said anything about banishment." His ears wobbled in agreement.

Nani in turn hesitated, her ears twitching ever so slightly. "Oh... what were you going to recommend?"

Tibit replied, "A visit to Santa, of course!"

Nani and Tibit looked at one another. Both were embarrassed and confused. All four ears seemed to swivel independently, from the direction of their mate to the opposing set of ears trying to determine who was confusing whom. Nani tried to figure out how and why she jumped to the banishment choice. Tibit now wondered if he should have reached that decision.

Nani recovered first. "Santa?" She said out loud to herself as she absorbed the thought. The more she thought about it the less sure she was about which was worse. A visit with Santa certainly was not banishment, but elves prided themselves on remaining unnoticed, for a lifetime if possible. Being singled out and acknowledged by others was never an elf's goal. In fact, quite the opposite was true. From an elf's perspective never being noticed, especially by Santa, meant you lead a successful life. However this was generally acknowledged to be nonsense since Santa already knew everyone anyway. But elves had no memory of a single elf ever going unnoticed for a lifetime. In practicality, if an elf had gone unnoticed, who would have known? The point being elves do not like having attention cast upon themselves.

Tibit shrugged. "I think that is the best course of action." He carried his book on humans back to its place on the shelf. As he regained his composure, he continued, "Distracted elves are more Santa's expertise. I'm used to common complaints related to interactions between species, especially Gnomes who as you know are generally regarded as stubborn, independent, poorly mannered, and smelly (probably from eating flies and earth worms)."

Nani rolled her eyes. She thought to herself impatiently, 'more about gnomes?'

Tibit, oblivious to Nani's reaction continued in the most authoritative tone, "They have a unique outlook on life in which everything that could go wrong will go wrong. Even if the thing goes right, there must be something wrong. Gnomes believe elves are too busy working, helping, fixing, and building things. Elves don't need to explore like gnomes. (Tibit spit out the word 'explore' with all its negative connotations). Elves like being part of a group, cooperating with and helping others. Generally being nice."

Tibit returned to his perch behind his desk, unaware that Nani's patience was wearing thin. "Fairies, on the other hand, offer a different type challenge in that they are obsessed with being perfect and are tireless nuisances. They believe elves are too serious and gnomes too dirty."

He looked up and noticed Nani's ears rhythmically tapping either side of her head. He decided to stop speaking, but his mind continued and convinced himself more experienced assistance was the right course of action. Before bothering Santa though he thought perhaps he should meet with Jojo first to fully understand the situation. He would hate to escalate this to the Big Man before he had fully investigated it. It may be nothing, after all. It could simply be a few too many sugar plums. Sugar plums in excess were certainly disruptive to his own system.

"Please bring Jojo here after dinner, so I can meet her before making my final recommendation."

Nani bowed slightly and went to find Jojo.

6. Elfish Mistakes

The hum of the assembly room began to grow. Unconsciously Jojo's hands began to work. She picked up a doll from the Body Bin, installed the joints that would allow the arms and legs to move, quickly added the head and then placed the completed form into the Assembled Bin. She completed one doll every forty-three seconds. Occasionally, her hand would slip and she lost a little time but catch up after a string of several smooth assemblies. She didn't think about much, which is common for elves. She simply performed her job gladly without complaint, care, frustration, or boredom. This is what elves did, every day, except Christmas day. Christmas day is a difficult one for elves because they don't have work to occupy themselves. As a result, a celebration was created to engage them. It includes dancing with fairies, staring contests with gnomes, and the traditional Candy Corn Spitting contest. Getting back to work the day after Christmas was always a great relief.

Jojo had performed her job with greater accuracy over the previous ten years, beginning in this position on her fifty-fifth birthday. The previous fifty-four years were filled with learning the colors of the rainbow, the proper way to drink something fizzy without burping, and honing her skills repairing broken toys.

Her fifty-fifth birthday though brought her the best birthday present any elf could get: her first job. She woke up several minutes early on that day being too excited to sleep, rushed through her Sassafras tea with eight lumps of sugar accompanied by a bowl of pink cotton candy then hurried off to work. She had received an engraved assignment letter congratulating her. She had not received any instructions on what to do when she reached her assigned room but intuitively began helping out where help was needed. Elves are able to fix anything so the idea of an assigned role was unnecessary. Elves with smaller hands tended to work on more detailed tasks while taller elves worked on things that were higher off the ground. Like a bird building a nest Jojo found a need each day, whatever it was, and filled it. Based on her size, dexterity, and experience, she tended toward assemblies. Other days might include packing completed dolls or cleaning up (although cleaning up was rarely necessary as elves are naturally very neat). She couldn't have been happier.

Upon her next birthday, her sixty-fifth, she would move on to one of the other rooms. Jojo did not know why elves changed rooms every 10 years. As far as she knew it was simply a tradition. Nor did it really matter to Jojo to which room she was assigned, she only had a desire to be helpful and productive.

Jojo did have a deeper secret though that she had not revealed to anyone, not even herself. Curiosity. She dreamt about other jobs. She wanted to be a Features elf and looked forward to the days when there was that need. To ask why would be the same as asking why someone preferred the color orange to blue. In the meantime Jojo knew she would spend the remainder of her sixty-fourth year working in this room, leaving only to eat, sleep and rejoice in being a productive and efficient elf. There was no time or desire for being bad or mean. There was only time for being an elf.

Something made Jojo stop and look around. All the other elves had also paused. The only movement and sound in the room was that of the machinery thumping rhythmically. She slowly realized all eyes were directed at her. She looked down and froze.

The room's main door opened. Nani walked in and stopped short. Her eyes followed the direction of the other elves' which landed squarely on Jojo. Instead of assembling dolls Jojo had been taking the arms, legs and heads off and putting them back into their respective bins. Nani assessed the situation and quickly walked over to the new elf. She touched Jojo's bowed head. Jojo was utterly humiliated. Nani gently but firmly guided her out of the room. As soon as Jojo relinquished her seat, another elf took her place and began to reassemble the dolls. The buzz rapidly returned to the room and production resumed. The incident, however, was not soon forgotten.

After exiting the room and shutting the door Nani paused and turned to Jojo. "Are you okay? What happened?"

"I... I don't know. One minute I was putting the arms on the bodies and the next I was removing the head." Her eyes began to fill with tears.

Nani gently took the little elf's hand and led her back to her room.

7. A Short Walk

Jojo rested the remainder of the afternoon in her room. Nani brought her some hot chocolate with two extra marshmallows to help her relax. Jojo remained silent, trying to understand why this was happening to her. Why was she so distracted? Would she be allowed to return to work? Was she in trouble? She had no answers for any of the many questions that raced through her mind.

After dinner, Nani came to Jojo's room, as she did every evening. Still shaken by the day's events, Jojo tried to calm herself and asked hopefully, "Story time?"

"Not tonight." Nani replied.

"Why?" Jojo asked, troubled.

"There's someone I'd like you to meet."

"Who?"

"His name is Tibit. He is a friend who is going to help us get you sorted out."

Jojo relaxed a little. 'Normal' was all she wanted, whatever it took. Jojo then asked hesitantly "Am I in trouble?"

"No. Of course not. Well, not really... I'm not sure." Nani realized she was not helping and tried to collect her own thoughts. She sat beside Jojo on her stone slab bed and put an arm around Jojo's shoulder. Nani touched Jojo's ears reassuringly. "This is a unique situation. It may be nothing at all. We just want to make sure you are feeling all right and have not come down with a mild case of brain freeze."

Jojo forced a smile.

"We need to visit someone who can help." Nani stood up and held out her hand. Jojo took it gratefully and stood up. They walked together out of the little elf's sleep chamber.

The North Pole complex was located completely under the polar ice. Constructed during a time before anyone could remember, a collection of caverns connected by an elaborate series of tunnels. Originally it had been above ground located on a lush green open plain built of wood and stone. Over the centuries as the climate cooled, slowly covering it with snow and ice. Gnomes were generally credited with much of the digging even though it was mostly the result of their foraging for grubs. The construction was completed with some help from friendly trolls and a touch of fairy dust. The gnomes asserted that the elves never even noticed the change from green grassy plain to ice as they were too busy with their work to be bothered by what was going on outside their work areas. The elves simply accepted the ice covered shelters as if they had always been so.

The tunnels were built with thick blocks of ice that were brightly lit with curved ceilings that merged into the walls on either side. There was no obvious means of lighting other than the tunnel itself which seemed to glow with a brilliant luminescence. The walls featured intricately decorated geometric patterns framing images of historic significance that at times looked almost whimsical. They included carvings of unicorns, lions with wings, and hairy elephants. The carvings were embedded behind the walls' perfectly smooth surface. Their transparency and depth made the images look three dimensional.

The elves took full credit for the beautiful and intricate decorations that made the tunnels and caverns their home. Before Christmas there were other holidays for which they prepared and that were reflected in the designs. These centered on the celestial seasons when the Elf Queen Star rose in the early evening sky to gently kiss the Bear constellation's nose. The color was mostly white for practical purposes but like the work rooms the tunnels captured all the colors of a rainbow. The bright color combinations and sweeping designs reflected nature and the Northern Lights, but the structure and symmetry reflected the elves own sense of order. Blending of colors was carefully controlled and designed. A debate raged for centuries whether or not pink and peach were actually the same color. A southern leprechaun who came for a visit almost settled the dispute when he arrived carrying a flower that had both colors in the same petal. The debate continued though because the purists argued that since they were in the same petal they were in fact the same color. The radicals contended that because the colors could be distinguished from either other they were, by the laws of nature, two separate colors. The debate continues to this day.

None of this was of interest to most elves who largely took the tunnels' art for granted. Elves typically walk directly from one place to another in the most efficient manner. They accept things as they are, do what is expected of them, ask no questions and discourage change. Jojo on the other hand couldn't resist looking at the carvings with great curiosity as she had not been in this part of the complex before.

8. You Be the Judge

The Interspecies Relations office door creaked as Nani pushed it open. Tibit's head snapped up from his nap. He appeared not to have moved since Nani last left. His ears rocked back and forth for a second getting their bearings from the abrupt movement of their host's head. Tibit leaned back and sized up the new elf. Nothing remarkable about her appearance, he thought, sharp features, nice sheen to the skin, toes and ears becoming more pointed as expected for her age.

He cleared his throat and tried to be pleasant and reassuring. "Come in. Come in. Have a seat."

Jojo marveled at the books and relatively bland appearance of the office. The colors were muted, the light was neutral and the room was quiet. Overall an uninteresting room, remarkable only for its lack of anything... remarkable.

Tibit continued, "Jojo, it's good to meet you. Nani has been telling me a little about you." Both Jojo and Tibit looked at Nani, then back at one another. "She tells me you have been having some...er... thoughts lately."

Jojo looked up at Nani then back to Tibit. "Well, not really thoughts, just a little trouble concentrating."

"Yes, I have already heard about the incident in the work room earlier. Word spreads quickly, you know. But not to worry, I'm sure it's happened before to other elves." Tibit knew full well that was an exaggeration. There had always been rumors of mistakes occurring as a result of too much help from other elves. The human phrase 'too many cooks in the kitchen' was a close analogy. But a case of simple distraction had never been recorded as far as Tibit knew. "It's something you will likely grow out of as you change into a mid elf." However, privately he was not so sure of this himself.

Jojo relaxed, slightly relieved. Nani remained rigid suspecting Tibit had stretched the truth.

Tibit continued, "Tell me about what has been distracting you."

Jojo replied, "I ask Nani lots of questions." She shifted her gaze between the two older elves.

Tibit assured her, "As you should while you develop your work skills." Then leading Jojo to the heart of the matter. "Was there a particular question that troubled you?"

Jojo's forehead furrowed as she concentrated on what question she could have asked that would be of concern? The events in the doll room had made her completely forget her question the night before. Her ears leaned forward as if to help her concentrate in her effort to remember. "I'm sorry, I don't recall."

Tibit was caught a little off guard. How could this question be forgotten? A rather fundamental belief to their own existence. He looked between Jojo and Nani. "The question was I believe, 'Are humans real?'"

"Oh, that question." She relaxed a little and spoke rapidly, "I was pretty tired and a little anxious about keeping up at work. I didn't mean any disrespect but it occurred to me how odd humans are compared to elves and that I didn't know anyone who had actually ever seen one."

Tibit became rigid. He was perplexed. The mere thought of questioning the existence of humans brought the purpose of elves into question. Unheard of, unspeakable, unthinkable and utterly confusing. And yet this little elf blurts it out as if she were attaching wheels on a train. His ears were motionless. Tibit leaned forward and pronounced in a very even but firm tone, "But that's just it. They are real."

Jojo perked up. "Are they like they are described in the stories? Are they round and stubborn and mean?"

"Well of course they are!" Tibit replied.

Jojo became more animated, "What was it like?"

"What was 'what' like?"

"The humans. How big were they? Did any of them talk to you?"

Tibit leaned back on his stool and chuckled quietly. "My dear little elf, I've never seen a human myself. That's just nonsense."

Jojo paused and looked intently at the senior elf. "You've never seen a human?"

"Of course not. But I don't need to see a human to know they are real." He replied in a condescending tone. He glanced at Nani, smirked, and then returned his attention to Jojo. "What they are like is already written in the books. What more do I need to know?"

"So... you have never seen a human?" Jojo repeated, warily.

"No one has. It's neither necessary nor practical," Tibit declared matter-of-factly.

"Then how do you know they are real?"

Tibit was stunned. Jojo and Tibit looked at one another in equal disbelief. Jojo was increasingly convinced she was right, Tibit was increasing convinced Jojo was unwell, and Nani stood by in utter confusion.

After a moment or two Tibit concluded "Well," clearing his throat, "I believe a visit to Santa is in order don't you?" His ears wobbled in agreement.

9. Who Are You?

Tibit, Jojo and Nani stood in front of the large red door. Twice as large as any Jojo had ever seen. A sign over it simply read "Santa." Nani had tagged along as she was responsible for Jojo's wellbeing. Tibit assured Nani it was not necessary but yielded under her stern glare. Now Tibit turned the brightly polished brass door knob and gave the door a push. It swung open silently. Tibit did not enter Santa's office but instead held out his hand ushering Jojo ahead. Jojo looked into the room, then at Nani. Nani was unsure what to do but realized this was beyond her training and control. She gently reached over and rubbed Jojo's ear. Tibit seemed nervous and cast furtive glances around Santa's office while remaining just outside the threshold. He was anxious to leave, so he began mumbling something about a recent troll problem that needed prompt attention and suggested Jojo hurry along so he could get back to his busy schedule.

Jojo stepped gingerly into the room and Tibit shut the door behind her. They were gone. Jojo looked around the room. She was not nervous but instead her curiosity got the better of her. Santa's office was darker than any room she had seen before, even darker than Tibit's office. Lit only by the tiny lights on the large Christmas tree in the corner and a fire in the fireplace which cast flickering shadows on the wood paneled walls. There was a very large, heavy wooden desk on one side of the room with intricately carved legs and covered with papers scattered around a massive book lying open in front of a large chair. The desk was surrounded floor to ceiling with stacks of paper leaning at incredibly awkward angles. Each looked about ready to tumble over and, like a domino, take all the other stacks down with it. The papers stuck out of the stacks at all different angles and were of all variety of shapes, colors and sizes. The office looked like a colorful forest of peppermint sticks. Without thinking she slowly moved to the middle of the room instinctively avoiding the stacks of paper, which she thought might very well crush her if one fell on her. There were shelves on one wall overflowing with odds and ends. The room appeared to be in a total state of confusion except for a round table by the fireplace on top of which sat a small plate of cookies and a glass of milk. The table was as tall as her.

An ancient oversized wooden rocking chair sat beside the table. She silently walked over and touched the arm making the chair rock forward. It squeaked painfully making her jump. Her ears reflexively squeezed themselves shut. True to her elfish instinct she rocked the chair slowly back and forth making it squeak again so she could assess the cause, stopping only after she figured out the needed repair. Her ears cautiously uncurled once the noise ceased. Jojo turned her attention to the rest of the room and concluded that all the other furniture also needed repair.

Unsure what to do next she decided to sit in the chair while she waited. She had to pull herself up into it. Once there, her legs dangled freely over the edge of the seat. She thought that maybe she would offer to help Santa with the furniture after their chat. "Chat" was the word Tibit used when he escorted her to the room. The way he used the word though puzzled Jojo. He seemed to pick the word very carefully as if he intended to say something different, changing his word choice at the last second. As he departed he wished her good luck almost as if he were saying farewell. That made her more uncertain than anything else he had said up to that point. Why would she need good luck? The chair began to squeak as she considered this.

The door to the room burst open. Jojo jumped, her eyes grew large, and her ears stood at attention as she looked upon Santa for the very first time. He was exactly like the pictures in the books she had read but much, much bigger, especially for an elf. He wore white socks, no shoes, a red shirt with white buttons and red pants held in place by two candy cane colored straps that ran over his shoulders and down his back. He had a broad belly and broader smile. He chuckled merrily.

Looking down at her he exclaimed, "Jojo! It is sooo nice to meet you. I don't get to see as many elves these days as I would like, especially the new elves. In fact, if I didn't know better, I would say they try to avoid me." He rested his hands on either side of his immense belly and let loose a loud and joyful "Ho, ho, ho!"

Jojo smiled wondering why she had been nervous. She was unable to take her eyes off of him. How did he get to be so big?

"Would you care for a cookie? Perhaps something sweeter? I am sure I can find whatever it is you might want."

Jojo was unable to respond. She was overwhelmed by the figure standing in front of her.

Santa softened a little, "Do you feel all right? There's no need to be frightened. You look a little pasty. I think some hot chocolate would do you good." He walked over to the fireplace and picked up a dark metal tea pot sitting on the fireplace hearth. He poured some dark rich liquid into a mug that was sitting beside it, turned and held it down to her.

Jojo continued to simply stare. She could not take the mug as she was mesmerized by the being in front of her. The squeaking chair was now silent.

Santa remained motionless for a few seconds as he waited for her to take the mug. Santa then began to smile, then giggle, then chuckle, finally breaking out into a full blown belly laugh. Coco sloshed out of the mug he was holding. His was not a spiteful or mocking type of laugh, but a pure and joyful laugh. The longer Jojo remained frozen

the louder he laughed, and the louder he laughed the more captivated Jojo became, her eyes grew wider by the second and her ears
stood up straight. His laughter had a calming effect on Jojo and
she began to laugh as well.

So there they were, Santa towering over the tiny elf, each looking at the other, laughing. Santa finally tried to catch his breath
and his laughter faded, but the smile never left his face. Jojo took
the oversized mug of coco from Santa and began to sip. She stared
at him from over its edge wondering what was going to happen
next.

Santa sat down in a wooden arm chair a few feet away, put his
hands on his knees and asked, "So tell me, to what do I owe this
honor?"

Jojo's head cocked a little to one side and looked at him
blankly.

Santa clarified, "That is, the honor of your visit?"

Jojo thought for a second, her face twisted slightly in confusion and replied, "I'm not really sure."

Santa's heavy white eyebrows rose momentarily. "Well according to this note from Tibit—a funny old elf don't you think?—it
seems there is some concern about your...let's say...recent behavior."

He leaned forward in his chair, coming nearer the little elf and
continued in a softer voice, "But between you and me I think it's a
bit of nonsense." He sat back in his chair and relaxed. Jojo did not
reply but simply continued to look at him.

"What's really going on is the other elves are threatened by
you."

Jojo's expression changed to a surprised stare. She thought to
herself. 'Threatened? By me?'

"Whether you noticed it or not," Santa continued, "elves don't like change or nonconformity. It makes them nervous because it makes them think about things differently. Don't get me wrong, elves can be very clever and industrious but they also rely on consistency in order to make sense of everything. Even if something is as clear as day." Santa explained, waving his arms broadly with a grand gesture. "If it causes them to do things differently, that makes them nervous, so they try to prevent it." He shook his head slightly, then smiled gently at Jojo. "And you seem to have caused a ripple in the elfin universe as it were."

Jojo did not understand a single thing he had just said. She did not know what a 'universe' was, but sat still trying to be polite. The more she thought about it though, causing other elves discomfort made her feel bad. Her stomach began to hurt, her toes curled, and her ears drooped down like a big gust of wind had caught them from behind. Her eyes dropped to the floor in front of her. "But I didn't mean to do anything wrong."

"Wrong? My dear, no one said you did."

Jojo continued to look at the floor in front of her pointed feet, convinced that she had done something terrible.

Santa tried to reassure her, "Let's back up a little. Why don't you tell me what happened?"

Jojo wasn't really sure where to begin. She felt very small. She held her breath for a second while she tried to find her courage. It seemed innocent enough but suddenly it felt ugly. She twitched in her seat wondering how to begin. She looked at the backs of her hands reluctant to repeat the question that had upset Nani and Tibit so much. She knew she was in trouble and was surely headed straight for the naughty list. When she looked up at Santa's bright face though she felt reassured by his kind and gentle smile so she replied, "I think it's because my mind wanders and I ask too many questions."

"What sorts of questions?"

Jojo hesitated then blurted out the thing that seemed to cause so much trouble but for which she still was desperate to receive an answer, "Are humans real?"

Santa's eyes opened a little wider. He leaned back and sat up as straight as his age would allow. Jojo pushed herself farther back into the chair. His smile began to grow. His whiskers straightened and his eyes squinted. Santa looked straight into, and then through Jojo, as if staring deep into space. He spoke more to himself than to Jojo. "What a strange, wonderfully odd question."

Santa continued to stare vacantly. Minutes passed. Finally Santa refocused on Jojo and asked, "What made you think of that?"

She again hesitated then replied, "I'm not sure. I just began to think as I heard the Christmas story. It occurred to me that humans seem very strange. Why were some of them mean and greedy? What would it be like to meet one? Then I realized I had never seen one."

"Interesting.... Have any of your friends suggested such a thing? Did you discuss it with others?"

"Of course not. My mind may wander but I'm not stupid." She smiled sheepishly. Santa returned the smile.

"But you asked your monitor elf, Nani, I believe?"

"Well, yes. But I ask her lots of things." Jojo paused "I didn't mean to do anything wrong."

Santa replied, "Of course not. But you are right, this type of question would not be well received by other elves." He pulled lightly at his white beard as he continued to think to himself.

Jojo hesitated then asked, "Am I in trouble?"

Santa's looked at Jojo "No. Of course not.... But we need to decide what to do with you."

"Do with me? Can't I just go back to be with the other elves and Nani?"

"I'm not sure that is wise. Not just yet anyway." He stood up and walked over to the fireplace. He picked up the fire poker and absent-mindedly pushed the burning logs around, sending sparks up the chimney like little fire flies escaping from a glass jar.

Jojo screwed up as much courage as she had left and blurted out, "So, are they?"

Santa twisted around to look at Jojo. "Are 'who' what?"

"Are humans real?"

Santa smiled again, "Well, of course, they're real."

Jojo sat silent, unconvinced.

When she did not respond, Santa swung his arm around, the poker cutting the air like a sword, and point at the stacks of paper. "See all these letters? Who do you think wrote them?"

Jojo looked more closely at the paper forest and realized they must be Christmas letters from the children. Hundreds of thousands of them, from hundreds of thousands of children. Human children. Santa took a step and grabbed one, pulling it from the middle of the stack closest to him. The stack rocked precariously as Santa handed the letter over to Jojo. A crudely drawn green Christmas tree decorated the red piece of paper, highlighted with smudges of blue, yellow, and gold crayon marks. Big uneven block letters spelled the name 'Pat.'

Jojo examined the picture for a few moments before looking back at Santa.

Santa then asked, "What do you think I am, after all?"

Jojo was dumbstruck not understanding the question.

Santa noted her confusion and added, "Jojo, I am a human."

He had always been referred to as the "jolly old elf," so Jojo had simply assumed he was just that. He looked very much like the pictures in the elfin text books but now that she saw him for herself she realized he did not look much like an elf at all, or at least not like any elf she had seen before. She had assumed Santa was from a different elf clan or some other similar explanation.

A slight tear traced down her cheek. She was sad that she had doubted everything she had been told. Sad that she had doubted Nani. Sad that she had questioned Santa. She felt horrible and wanted to melt away into the floor, disappear into a cloud and go unnoticed for evermore.

Santa walked over, picked up Jojo from the rocker and sat in the chair putting Jojo on his lap. He gently rested his gloved hand in the middle of her back, rubbing ever so slightly. Jojo relaxed, wishing the moment would never end. They sat together staring into the flickering flames of the fire and listening to the rhythmic ticking of a large clock hidden somewhere in the room.

"You know Jojo, you are a very special elf."

Jojo remained motionless.

"You have a great gift."

10. What's Wrong with Them?

Jojo listened distantly to Santa's reassurances but did not believe him. He was surely exaggerating and simply trying to comfort her. 'Gift,' ha! What gift was it that caused her to question and doubt? A gift she would happily give back but didn't know how.

"Santa?" She asked gazing into the slowly burning fire.

"Yes, Jojo?"

"Will I be able to go back to work?"

"If that's what you want, then yes."

"What do you mean, if that's what I want?"

"Exactly that. If you want to go back to the work rooms you are more than welcome to do that." He paused then added, "But..."

"'But?'"

"But you won't be able to go back to who you were before."

Jojo lifted her head and looked at Santa. "What do you mean?"

Santa shifted his gaze from the fire to Jojo, "There is something that happens when you question things. Your mind opens and you lose your ability to believe unconditionally."

Jojo blinked, remaining focused on Santa.

"You see Jojo, elves have a strong ability to simply 'believe.' There is no right or wrong. No 'ifs' or 'buts'. There is only acceptance of themselves, acceptance of each other, and acceptance of what they do. They believe in who they are and what they do in its most basic form their whole lives. It keeps them happy and they have no reason to change. Humans also have the ability to believe," Santa sighed, "but mostly only while they are young. Humans never lose this ability but as they grow older they begin to forget how to believe unconditionally. They question their beliefs." He stopped rocking and looked closely at the elf in his lap, "Do you understand?"

Jojo remained silent then shook her head from side to side indicating she did not.

Santa looked back at the fire and began rocking, the chair squeaked lightly in rhythm with the ticking clock. "What I try to do every Christmas is to extend humans' desire to believe. The real gift of Christmas is allowing them to relive that state of innocence for just a little longer. For another week, month or even a year until the next Christmas, if possible, because each day they believe, they will remain happy. But in the end humans begins to question more and more things, challenging their beliefs and minimizing the importance of innocence and true happiness. As they grow older they begin to lose sight of the most important things in life."

Santa's voice drifted off and sat quietly.

"Does this cause them to be naughty?"

Santa nodded, "Unfortunately, yes."

Jojo sat up a little, "But why are children mean and greedy before they grow up? Why is there a naughty and nice list?"

"Naughty children are the ones who want to grow up before they should. Keeping the list helps to teach them of the consequences of growing up." Santa smiled a devilish smile and whispered, "But to be honest, no child remains on the naughty list for very long. They can't be nice all the time. That too is in their human nature. But they also have the ability to be exceptionally nice."

Jojo thought for a moment, "If they all become mean in the end, why bother?"

Santa brightened, "Because they never lose the ability to believe. The possibility that they can remember to trust and believe remains with them always. It's my job to help them to do just that: Believe."

11. The Mrs.

The door swung open and in walked a large round woman carrying a tray. Her white hair flowed around her head like a small snow storm held in check by a loosely tied red scarf. She wore a matching red robe with white fringe that fully covered her ample size. On her feet were red slippers with a little bell on each toe. She marched into the room walking directly to the fireplace and stopped beside Santa and Jojo sitting in the chair. She bent over and held the tray down so Jojo could see what it held. There were cookies of all shapes and colors. Jojo glanced at the tray but had to look back up at Mrs. Claus. Her eyes were bright blue and her smile stretched from ear to ear.

"Here, dear. Take a cookie. Two will make you feel even better," she said, winking.

Jojo carefully took a cookie from the top of the pile without taking her eyes off Mrs. Claus. She absentmindedly nibbled its edge while she gazed up at the woman in front of her.

"You might not know it, but we don't get many elf visits." She shifted her eyes and looked at Santa, her smile shrinking slightly while continuing to speak to Jojo "The elves seem to be afraid of us." Santa's eyes dropped to the floor to avoid Mrs. Claus' stare. Mrs. Claus returned her attention to Jojo and her smile returned. "So we are very glad to have you come visit us."

Jojo didn't know what to say so she took another small bite of her cookie.

"So what brings you here?" Mrs. Claus asked, bent slightly at the waist looking intently at Jojo.

"Jojo came to ..." Santa began but quickly stopped as Mrs. Claus, without removing her eyes from Jojo, held up her hand.

Santa cleared his throat as if he had swallowed a bug and leaned back into the chair.

"You were saying, dear?" Mrs. Claus asked, still looking at Jojo.

Jojo glanced over to Santa then back to Mrs. Claus. She remained silent, not entirely sure how to answer. After a brief pause Santa leaned forward and sheepishly whispered in his wife's ear, "She doesn't believe in humans."

Mrs. Claus' eyes grew wide and her whole face became a large smile. "What a curious thought. My dear that is the most adorable thing I have heard in a long time."

Jojo remained speechless.

Mrs. Claus continued, "Where did you get that idea?"

Jojo swallowed the bit of cookie in her mouth and replied, "Because no one has ever seen one."

Mrs. Claus looked at Santa and stated firmly, "You see what happens when you don't invite guests over to visit? They get these strange notions about things simply out of ignorance." Santa's face reddened in embarrassment. Mrs. Claus looked back at Jojo. "I've been telling him for years that we needed to mingle more with the elves but he would not have it. Some nonsense about 'distracting them because they seemed so busy'." She looked back to Santa, "It seems like you were able to distract them well enough as it is."

Santa looked at Mrs. Claus with a quizzical expression, not quite sure how this turned out to be his fault.

Mrs. Claus continued speaking to Santa, "You can't keep people or elves in the dark and expect them to understand everything."

Santa tried to defend himself, "But I thought somethings didn't need to be explained. I thought everyone already knew."

Mrs. Claus looked at Jojo and smirked, "This is quite the introduction to dealing with humans. What other notions did you have about Santa? That he was perfect, or perhaps all knowing?" She shook her head back and forth and redirected her gaze to Santa. "Men. They would like us to think so." She looked back at Jojo and again winked, "But we know better."

Jojo was not sure what to make of that comment so instead blurted out, "I always assumed Santa was an elf."

Mrs. Claus gave Santa a stern look. Santa tried to lighten the mood and chuckled, "As you can see I am a bit oversized for an elf."

"Nor does he have the temperament." Mrs. Claus added under her breath.

Jojo's ears leaned forward and she asked, "But if you are a human, why do you live here?"

He smiled, glanced at Mrs. Claus whose stern look was beginning to diminish, and then looked back at Jojo. With a slight shrug he added, "It is a little complicated."

12. Movement

Jojo lay on the hearth in front of Santa's fireplace. It was getting late. Mrs. Clause decided Jojo should spend the rest of the night with them. 'She only needs an hour of sleep anyway', Mrs. Claus reminded herself.

The Clauses provided Jojo several small blankets to lie on, not realizing that the new elf preferred a hard surface. A dusty rag doll with bright red hair was pulled from the shelf for use as a pillow. One of the black button eyes was loose, held on by a single thread. Mrs. Claus carefully removed it and put it in her pocket for safe keeping so it wouldn't get lost. The Clauses tucked Jojo in as best as they knew how and left her alone. The light from the fire flickered hypnotically but try as she might Jojo couldn't fall asleep. She rolled onto her back and stared at the ceiling. Her mind was full of distractions.

For the first time she could remember she was unable to go to sleep. The ceiling twinkled with little lights that looked like stars imagining they were real, but she knew they were only Zips reflecting light causing them to sparkle like ice. Zips are extremely delicate and vanish instantly if touched. No one really knows what happens to them but fanciful creatures such as Jojo were taught at a very early age not to grab them for fear of injuring them. In reality, they are faster than gnomes and the illusion of glittering is reflected light when they stop moving.

"So humans are real." Jojo whispered to herself. Everything she had been told was true. She relaxed believing things would soon go back to normal. She felt silly for even entertaining the thought they didn't exist. She had not anticipated the other bit of news that Santa was also a human but in retrospect it sort of made sense. She now assumed Mrs. Claus was human as well. How many other humans were there? Where were they? Did they all look like Santa? The seemingly simple question that started this whole excitement was being replaced with more questions. She needed to calm down and get some sleep or she wouldn't be ready for work the next day... Would she go to work the next day? Surely she would be allowed ....

Something moved near the Christmas tree in the corner of the room. Shadows covered the tree making it hard to see. Even in the dark Jojo could tell the tree was elaborately decorated, covered with all sorts of shiny ornaments. Many of them appeared to be either very old, poorly made, or both. If nothing else she had an eye for quality, which these ornaments lacked. There were hand painted wooden animals, shiny metallic balls, glass beads, and even paper chains. Zips had attached themselves to the branches flashing in irregular patterns making the tree sparkle. These flickered in a variety of colors according to the type of Zip. The most common color is a yellow-gold, making them appear to be lightning bugs when seen from a distance. Occasionally red and blue can also be found farther south where it is warmer. It is believed Zips attaching themselves to tree branches is the origin of putting lights on Christmas trees. At the top of Santa's tree was a star that leaned a little to one side. It dimly reflected enough of the firelight so she could make out its shape. She stared at it wondering why it was haphazardly placed.

There, something moved again, but this time she focused on the base of the tree. Scattered around the tree were packages covered in all sorts of paper and ribbons. Some were ripped open, others remained pristine and untouched. Jojo realized what troubled her about this room. Things seemed out of place and disorderly. This was not the way elves did

things. Everything has a place and a purpose, like a toy train with many pieces that precisely fit together. What was it about Santa that allowed his room to end up like this? Were all humans this messy?

The thing near the base of the tree was not moving now but as she surveyed the wreckage surrounding the tree it reminded her of those pictures in which you search to find hidden objects. The trick, she learned early on, was to not look too hard. She unfocused her eyes and continued to scan the shadows looking for unusual patterns that didn't belong. The nose appeared first. She didn't immediately realize it was a nose but it looked odd which is what caught her eye. As she continued to stare she made out one of the ears and the tip of one foot. It seemed to be hiding behind one of the shredded boxes looking back at her.

She looked at it for a few more minutes before she rose and moved closer keeping her eyes firmly fixed on the spot. It remained motionless but a lone visible eye followed her every movement. She reached down, gently pulled back a piece of blue tissue paper and gold ribbon to unveil a gnome. It was only about a foot tall. He had a dirty round, pointed red hat pulled down tight over his head. He had a brown beard, fur jacket, thick brown belt, purple pants, and black leather boots. His skin looked as leathery as his boots and just as dirty. He did not move but remained perfectly still except for his eyes which continued to track Jojo as she squatted down to get a better look.

She reached over and poked his little round belly. He remained absolutely still. If he weren't so soft when she touched him she would have thought he was a statue. He looked very much like Schnug, the gnome she had befriended when she was younger, only this gnome was a little smaller. Jojo gently cleared her throat, "Hello."

He remained motionless.

"What's your name?" Jojo asked.

The gnome intently returned Jojo's gaze but remained perfectly still.

"What are you doing here?" she persisted.

A voice above her replied, "Don't you know he's not going to respond?"

Jojo quickly looked up in the direction of the voice. She heard a slight rustling at her feet, looked back down and the gnome was gone. The voice was a high pitched squeak. It came from somewhere near the top of the tree. She scanned the tree quickly, methodically moving her eyes from one side to the other, up a little, then back the other way.

"Didn't I tell you he wouldn't respond?"

Jojo's eyes immediately focused on the star.

"You know they don't like talking to strangers, right?" A piece of what she thought was the star floated down toward Jojo. A fairy landed on a nearby branch.

Jojo had only rarely seen fairies. On occasion they are called to make emergency repairs with their fairy dust such as the Christmas of 1961. That was the year when the conveyor belt broke down while loading the sleigh. Without repairs Norway and parts of Sweden would have missed a visit from Santa. Elves prided themselves on being able to fix anything without the use of magic and since the magical repair eventually wore off it felt like cheating. However in such cases exceptions can be made.

The fairy was small but glowed brightly as it sat on a tree branch at eye level with Jojo. The star atop the tree was no longer leaning so the fairy must have simply been sitting on it causing it to tilt to one side. The fairy shimmered like iridescent wrapping paper with transparent wings. It wore a tiny leaf around the waist tied with silk from a spider's web.

Jojo had never talked to a fairy before since they were not native to the North Pole. Besides being very suspicious and secretive folk, fairies had little interest in talking to elves since elves had no appreciation for the finer aspects of dance. Elves on the other hand were generally too busy for small talk. In short they each found the other uninteresting.

Jojo examined the fairy a few more seconds then cast her eyes about the room trying to spot the gnome again. Jojo mumbled a reply to fairy's question about gnomes' talking to strangers, yet more to herself, "But at least gnomes are interesting when they do talk."

13. Introductions

The only gnome Jojo had met before was Schnug. They had been in a young interspecies program together where fanciful creatures are introduced to each other. The term 'fanciful' is unpopular with elves, fairies, pixies and gnomes, not to mention trolls, dragons, and leprechauns. In other words, all non-humans. Originally all creatures were considered equal but over time humans began to think of themselves as superior. This caused the others to shun the humans, who in turn began to consider the others as not real and began to use the derogatory term 'fanciful.'

The goal of the program was to develop a mutual understanding among all creatures through interaction at a young age. The result was polite conversation but understanding was never truly achieved. The creatures were simply too different. Schnug and Jojo however liked one another from the start perhaps because of their differences. This was not typical and this apparent success instead caused concern among the teachers. It was 'not normal.' The teachers' concerns though were never marked into Jojo's records which in hindsight was probably a mistake.

Jojo found Schnug to be dirty, crude and mistrustful. When they were given a project to work on, Jojo immediately began figuring out the answer. Schnug wanted to know why they were given the project in the first place. When they had snacks Schnug was unwilling to eat until Jojo had taken a bite first, partly because of his fear of being poisoned, but mostly because gnomes dislike treats unless they are intensely sour. "The bitterer the betterer," he was known to say.

What the new elf and the gnome did have in common was curiosity. Gnomes are naturally curious but, unlike most elves, so was Jojo. They had many teacher-led conversations as part of the daily Topics to Discuss sessions. Between sessions Jojo and Schnug asked one another lots of questions and shared ideas on many things, one of which happened to be the existence of humans. Jojo found Schnug's ideas laughable but the seeds of doubt had been planted and in Jojo's curious mind they took root.

Without moving from her spot beside the tree Jojo scanned Santa's office. The shadows made for good hiding places. She surveyed the piles of paper and tried to see behind the clutter. Her ears swiveled in two independent directions on either side of her head trying to help to scan for any sound that might reveal the gnome. Then, up on the third shelf, between the music box and the plane with the broken propeller, there he was. He would have been a perfect little book end had there been a second gnome. He appeared to be a totally inanimate object of little note beside other unremarkable objects. They locked eyes. Now that he was found the gnome waited patiently for Jojo to look away so that he could dash to new hiding spot. Gnomes have an inherent contradiction in their personalities in that they desperately want to both see but remain unseen. Generations of practice resulted in this curious skill of hiding in the open.

Without taking her eyes off of the gnome Jojo asked the fairy, "What's his name?"

"Why do you need to know Bort's name?" the fairy countered.

Jojo sighed but maintained her focus on Bort. She recalled another reason why elves did not get along well with fairies: Fairies were very elusive and usually phrased their answers in the form a question. So when questions are answered with other questions it limited the amount of information actually exchanged and ultimately frustrated elves. Even so, Jojo noted the little bit of information that was provided and continued, "And what is your name?" she inquired of the fairy.

The fairy puffed her chest toward Jojo. "Don't you know I am named Frit?"

14. Circles

Fairy circles form during the summer months in old growth forests, remote grasslands or mist covered swamps far from curious onlookers or spies. A place where fairies congregated nightly between the spring and summer to dance and sing. Fairy circle participation was limited to individual families or 'queues.' Each queue jealously protects itself and its members from outsiders, including fairies from other queues. Common bonds were created among the queue during festivities that strengthened the dependence of each fairy upon the whole. Some queues could be quite large to include several hundred members but most averaged only a couple dozen fairies each.

Queues resemble bee colonies where there is a single queen who is the mother to the rest of the queue, which is comprised exclusively of females, making every member a sister to the other. But they are different in that they also have a head drone called a Tom-Tom (also a female) who manages the queue and maintains order and discipline. The queen and Tom-Tom are in complete control, and the rest of the queue obeys without question. Any disruption is punished quickly and severely, typically in the form of expulsion. In some rare cases expelled fairies are able to find other expelled fairies from different queues and form a new queue. Sadly though in most cases they simply disappear never to be seen again.

Frit had never been a typical fairy. She tried hard to learn the intricate fairy dances that included complicated choreographies, weaving in and around each other while flashing particular colors at precise intervals. But somehow she would end up in the wrong spot, out of rhythm, or flash the wrong color. None of the others seemed to have this problem. She always felt like she was on the outside looking in at the rest of her queue.

During the day fairies guard the woods around their home against intruders. Anyone who dared to wander into their domain was deemed a spy. Even if by complete accident on the part of the intruder. In a fairy's mind nothing was accidental. Intruders are quickly cast under a spell with fairy dust and led away to some other part of the wood or swamp where all spies would find themselves sometime later with no memory of fairies or even how they arrived at their present location. Naturally this experience would be disorienting but from the fairies' perspective it was the spy's own fault.

One day Frit was patrolling the woods trying to rehearse the dance moves from the previous night. She desperately wanted to avoid knocking down half a dozen of her sisters again. In her deep state of concentration she literally bumped into a great beast. The collision knocked Frit to the ground. The beast, what a human might recognize as a rabbit, just twitched its whiskers seemingly oblivious to the altercation. Frit, fully expecting to be attacked, remained motionless staring at the creature in fear and awe. After a few moments Frit found the courage to stand up. The rabbit's only response was to twist its ears searching for threats. A whisker thumped Frit on her side and knocked her back to the ground.

In her most authoritative voice Frit yelled up to the beast, "What are you doing trespassing in our realm?"

Naturally the rabbit did not respond or even recognize that a question was asked. It did hear a curious high pitched squeak which caused it to freeze except for its long brown ears that swiveled in search of the source of the noise trying to determine if danger lurked nearby.

"Don't you think you should leave immediately?"

It chewed the leaf already in its mouth a couple times then stopped again to listen, its ears turning in various directions to pick up any warning sounds. Suddenly it fell over on its side. Frit looked up. Tom-Tom's wings vibrated rapidly holding her position above the beast. Tom-Tom checked the beast to make sure it was completely unconscious then redirected her attention to Frit. Her hands rested on her hips as she looked disapprovingly at Frit.

"How could you let this spy into our midst?"

Frit remained speechless.

"Don't you realize the importance of perfect secrecy?"

Frit blinked, unable to respond.

"I think it's time we had a talk with the Queen, don't you?"

The series of events that followed were a blur. Out of pure kindness in the Queen's heart Frit was sent to the North Pole with a simple note addressed to Santa Claus. Whether Frit actually made it to the North Pole or not was not really a concern of the Queen or Tom-Tom because once Frit was beyond their territory the memory of her within the queue vanished as if she had never existed.

15. Lots of Questions

"What are you doing here?" Jojo asked Frit with open curiosity while keeping her eyes fixed on the gnome.

"Can't you see we live here?" Frit responded with a touch of annoyance

'Live here?' This was not what Jojo had expected. Her eyes reflexively glanced over Frit. She immediately realized her mistake and looked back to the bookcase. Sure enough, Bort was gone again. She smiled. This game was one she very much enjoyed playing with Schnug. Schnug would hide and Jojo would see how quickly she could spot him again. It was great practice for the two of them as they each developed their individual skills— Jojo's attention to detail and Schnug's ability to hide in the open. The game would go on until Jojo simply wore out, as gnomes are perfectly capable of falling asleep in their hiding position. The fond memory of those games came back to Jojo in this brief encounter, but the answer to her question was more interesting at this point. Taking a break from her search for Bort, she directed her attention to Frit.

"You live in Santa's office?" she asked Frit more directly.

"Didn't I already answer that?" Frit replied.

This evasive questioning style was difficult for elves. Elves practiced fairy speech but universally agreed that was impractical. Teachers recommended asking questions with simple answers if possible, but that didn't always work. Jojo tried to think through her questions a little more carefully. She took a breath to relax and tried again.

"Why do you live in Santa's office?"

Frit did not answer. To fairies, elves were much too direct. Elves wanted crisp, simple answers. The artful banter that made fairy speech universally loved by all, according to fairies anyway, was totally lost on elves. Elves were not able to appreciate the delicate linguistic nuances of the fairy's superior dialect.

Jojo tried again, "Are you in trouble?"

Frit's glow dimmed ever so slightly. "I'm not a good fairy," she replied softly, her wings drooped ever so slightly.

Jojo considered this for a few moments. The lack of a question in response suggested it was difficult for Frit, and Jojo tried to imagine what must of have happened, but she knew it must be serious. Jojo began to think about her own situation. She felt very alone. Her ears sagged forward and in a single motion Jojo sat down, cross-legged on the floor. She had no idea what would happen next. The fire crackled and flickered as Jojo stared at a wood knot in the floor just in front of her legs.

Something leaned against her shoulder. She looked over and was

surprised to find Bort leaning motionless against her. Even sitting, Jojo was taller than the gnome. Looking at the small figure she smiled weakly and said, "You are very fast Bort." She detected a slight curve in his lip as he held back a grin while staring directly ahead.

To a gnome, anything bigger than themselves is considered a predator. Gnomes' first line of defense is stealth which is a product of their speed and ability to time the predator's moment of distraction. A blink of an eye is all they need to relocate to new spot before resuming their hiding posture. A distracted glance or a turned head is more than enough time for a gnome to re-hide. For a Gnome moving at top speed everything around them appears to move in slow motion.

Frit fluttered down and perched on the top of Bort's hat. The three of them quietly observed each other. Jojo tried to grasp her new surroundings.

Frit broke the silence, "So, you don't believe in humans?"

Jojo realized that they had heard her whole conversation with Santa and with Mrs. Claus. The stress of the preceding hours had been more than Jojo had ever experienced. This moment of camaraderie helped her relax. "Yes... well, ... I didn't, ... but I do now."

Bort blurted out, "It's not the craziest thing I have ever heard." His voice was much too deep for his size. It sounded deeper even than Santa's. Jojo dared not react for fear Bort might be insulted somehow and hide again.

Frit looked down at Bort. "If anyone knows 'crazy' it's you." Frit again lost the typical fairy questioning pattern. Maybe this contributed to her being sent to live with Santa.

"What do you mean by that?" challenged Bort.

Frit's wings lifted her up to a hovering position eye level with Bort. "I've heard more wild ideas in the past few weeks than I have heard in my entire life. And you didn't even begin to really talk until five days ago!"

"Just because you are not as observant as I am does not make my stories less true." Bort reacted.

"Observant or a distorted sense of reality?" Frit returned.

Jojo began to think the fairy talked too much. Her experience with Schnug had been that although his ideas were different, they seemed to have some grain of truth in them, and besides, they were entertaining to consider.

Jojo interrupted. "What sort of ideas?"

Finally something other than Bort's eyes and mouth moved. His body remained rigid but rotated around toward Jojo. When he fully faced her, he replied, "Have you ever heard of a city with buildings so high you can't see their tops?"

Frit rolled her eyes mockingly. "Yes, of course, and there are no trees or animals except those behind metal fences."

Bort looked at Jojo, "And machines large enough to carry hundreds of people at a time?"

Frit shook her head with amused disbelief.

Jojo looked between Frit and Bort.

Frit flew closer to Jojo as if to tell her a secret but said loudly enough so Bort could hear, "Didn't I say he had a distorted sense of reality?"

Bort stiffened even more, "It's absolutely true. I have seen it." He shifted his eyes back and forth between Frit and Jojo.

"And I suppose no one can do magic or fly?" Frit smirked her question to Bort.

"I don't know about magic but they have machines that can fly higher than the clouds," he retorted.

"Where is this place?" Jojo asked, amazed by the concept. She had never heard of anything like this before, not even from Schnug.

"South," Bort said.

Jojo hesitated, "South?"

"Yes," asserted Bort.

"Where is South?" Jojo wondered aloud. "Can we see it from here?"

"'South is that way," Bort said, looking across the room, indicating the direction, "and it is very far, so, no, you can't see it from here."

"Why am I not surprised?" Frit mumbled.

Bort looked sternly at Frit, frustrated that she did not believe him.

The door swung open, and Santa stepped into the room. The conversation immediately stopped. Santa saw the three new acquaintances and smiled broadly.

"I see you have found each other," Santa exclaimed, standing over his guests. Compared to Santa they were all very small. Frit flitted to the fireplace mantel to be level with Santa's snowy white head. Jojo remained seated on the floor. The gnome remained hidden beside Jojo but his eyes strained to the top of his eye sockets trying to see the face of the big red predator standing above him. Although Bort knew Santa, Santa was still very large and someone of whom to be wary.

"I assume everyone has introduced themselves?" Santa asked.

Jojo hesitated then said, "Sort of."

"How far did you get?" he queried the new elf.

Frit broke in. "Bort was telling more of his tales to Jojo. And like a typical elf, she believed him."

Frit winked knowingly at Santa suggesting they both knew better and their superior intellect protected them from falling victim to such nonsense.

"Oh?" Santa asked with a grin. "Which tale is this?"

"The city with lights," Bort blurted out.

"You know," Frit interrupted sarcastically, "the one with the tall buildings, no trees, too many people to count, bad smells, and flying machines. Foolishness."

Santa looked at Frit, "But that is all true."

Bort's eyes widened, Jojo's ears stood up stiffly at attention and Frit glowed a little dimmer.

16. Caught Hiding

The three new acquaintances talked with Santa by the fireplace. Santa ate cookies and milk, Jojo was given her daily ration of candy, Frit absorbed the energy she needed from the fire, and Bort ate a millipede he found making its way across the floor.

Bort began telling stories he had either seen himself or heard from other gnomes. Santa noted occasional exaggerations but largely allowed Bort to weave his tales. Bort never sat, instead preferring his rigid standing position. He was quite entertaining as it turned out. The more he talked the more expressive his face and voice became. At one point he even used a couple of very slight hand gestures which everyone, including Bort, noticed. Bort turned red with embarrassment as the others laughed in a good spirited fashion.

Bort was the first in the group to live with Santa. He claimed to have been captured by a human on Christmas Eve and put in the human's house as a gift to another human. In truth he wasn't captured but instead was found hiding in the human's back yard. The human thought he was a run-of-the-mill, store-bought yard gnome and decided Bort would make a good gag gift for the human's younger brother. He picked up Bort without any effort because gnomes, though very fast, are extremely easy to catch if you don't take your eyes off of them. It's only when you look away that they disappear.

That night Santa stopped at the house to make his annual delivery. Santa filled the stockings by the fireplace and stopped for a cookie, his 123,659th of the night. Although the cookies looked delicious, the cook was not particularly skilled. The mother who made them used too much salt and left them in the oven too long. Santa thought to himself that maybe he should have given her that miniature oven when she was eight years old instead of the doll that wet itself. That's when Santa noticed Bort tied up with a ribbon. He immediately recognized the gnome for what he was and untied him. Santa listened attentively to Bort's tale of capture, knowing that by the next day he would once again be back outside and free to hide elsewhere.

Santa felt an odd connection to the gnome and offered to let him return to the North Pole with him. Bort, being naturally curious, accepted. He rode along while Santa finished his Christmas Eve deliveries. As they approached the North Pole Bort allowed Santa to put him into the now empty present sack. When they landed Mrs. Claus hustled Santa into the office for a nice cup of hot chocolate to warm up and relax. She pumped Santa for every detail of the trip as she did every year. When Santa reached the part related to Bort the gnome emerged from the sack. Mrs. Claus, anxious for some new companionship, insisted Bort stay for as long as he wanted. A month later Bort had yet to find a reason to leave and became a permanent guest. After all he was small, quiet, and helped keep the insect population under control with his constant snacking.

So here they were, a distracted elf, a sarcastic fairy, a poorly hidden gnome, and a fat old human. They sat the rest of the night listening to Bort's tall tales of places that didn't exist, Frit's reaction of utter disbelief, and Jojo's desire to believe the impossible.

Santa became aware of a curious camaraderie among his guests. The fanciful creatures were quite animated as they talked to each other and seemed to genuinely complement each other in unusual ways. He wondered to himself if this could this be the next threesome. Is this how it starts?

17. A Little Help

Santa interrupted his guests' lively debate comparing the texture and taste of grub worms to that of gummy bears.

"I need your help."

They stopped talking and looked at Santa. His eyes were fixed on the glowing embers in the fireplace. "Things are going to change around here and I need the three of you to help me."

They remained as motionless as a gnome.

"Change?" asked Jojo.

"I'm afraid so." Santa replied with a sigh.

"What does that mean?"

"Very soon I'll have to leave."

They simultaneously peppered him with questions, "Leave the North Pole?" "For how long?" "Where are you going?" "Can we come with you?" "Why?"

Santa appreciated the enthusiasm but held up both hands and cut them short. "Maybe it will help if I tell you my story," Santa suggested.

He told his story as well as he could remember, pulling from his earliest memories. As he spoke they sat stunned. Who would have guessed this was the eighteenth Santa, starting with Saint Nicholas in 292AD? Well, that wasn't exactly right. This was the eighteenth human host in which the Santa Spirit lived thus the term 'Christmas Spirit.' The 'Spirit' didn't change but the human body which hosted it eventually wore out and had to be replaced.

He described how the Santa Spirit coexisted with the host. Good spirits, like the Santa Spirit, are embraced by the host to form a single being. He elaborated on the concepts of free will, self-determination, and making good choices—none of which the three understood—but they did not want to interrupt him. In the case of Santa though, before the host's body dies, the Spirit must find a new host. But it can't be just any host. It has to be a human host with particular qualities that make it suitable for the Santa Spirit.

"What does this have to do with us?" Frit asked timidly.

Santa raised his eyebrows. He thought it seemed pretty obvious, "I need you to find the next host."

The trio blinked in unison.

Santa continued, "Who would be better to identify the host than the three of you?"

They were stunned. Who were they? Each was an outcast of some sort, ill-suited for the roles they thought they were born to be.

"I was not sure who was going to help me until just now. As I sit here observing you it's as obvious as the whiskers on my chin." He paused for a moment, "I'll admit I'm a little rusty on the details, after all the last time this happened was nearly eighty years ago and I was not involved in the search. What I do know is that I need help and you three seem like the perfect team to do it."

"But how can we find the host? Wouldn't another human be better suited to find a... replacement?" asked Bort.

Santa laughed, "Despite what you think about humans the one thing they are not good at is judging each other. They are too quick to jump to conclusions, form bad opinions, and can ultimately make bad decisions. Those opinions once made are very slow to change. No, it seems to me that other species are better suited to objectively evaluate humans."

They looked at each other, not really understanding any of this. Santa watched them for a few seconds, shrugged and added, "Besides, that is how it has always been done."

Jojo spoke first, "There must be some mistake. Even assuming we are able to find a human how would we know if he is a suitable host?"

"That's easy. First of all," Santa explained, "humans are not hard to find. Secondly you'll know it's the host if you all like him."

The three again responded with blank stares.

Santa continued as if speaking from a distant memory, "As I understand it there are enough differences between humans and all other species that a natural dislike exists, sort of like cats and dogs."

"What are cats and dogs?" Jojo asked.

"Never mind. The point is, if all of you like the same human, he will be a satisfactory host."

"That makes no sense." blurted out Frit, her wings vibrating behind her.

"And why us?" added Jojo, "We don't even get along with our own kind."

Bort took a very quick step closer to Santa and added, "I don't think we are the best choices. This is a big mistake."

"Nonsense! On the contrary, you have each been isolated from your own kind because of your willingness to interact with those unlike yourselves. Being open to new ideas makes you uniquely qualified. In turn, if you each like this individual it reveals his ability to effectively relate to a wide variety of species such as yourselves."

The three new friends exchanged suspicious glances.

"Is there only one possible host?" Jojo wondered aloud.

"No, but only a few are suitable and finding them among the billions of people on the earth could be a little tricky," Santa cautioned.

"Is a 'billion' more than a hundred?" Frit looked at him quizzically.

Santa smiled, "Yes. Quite a bit more than a hundred."

Jojo blurted out, "I wasn't even sure humans existed until a little while ago, and I certainly don't know how to find one. Yet now you want us to find the one in a billion? How could we possibly do that?"

"I'm glad you asked." Santa walked over to one of the shelves holding the broken toys and picked up a clear glass ball coated with dust.

He polished it briefly with his shirt sleeve and handed it to Jojo.

"With this."

Jojo took the heavy, unremarkable snow globe. Inside the globe was a miniature sleigh resting on a small, snow covered hill. A tiny reindeer stood at the ready in front of the sleigh. The sleigh was intricately detailed in every way including thin gold trim along the edges, buttons holding the seat cushion in place, and whisper thin reigns for the reindeer hanging loosely waiting for a driver. In the back of the sleigh was a single wrapped present. Jojo looked at it for a couple seconds then up at Santa with a confused look on her face.

Anticipating the question he added with a smile, "You need to give it a good shake first."

18. Deep Insight

Jojo looked at the glass ball and gave it gentle shake fearful she might break it. It caused the snow inside the globe to rise lightly then quickly settle again. She looked at it as Santa instructed. She concentrated hard. She squinted her eyes so they began to water, but nothing happened.

Santa touched her on the shoulder and calmly suggested, "Relax. Don't force it."

Jojo looked away shaking her head to remove the tension.

"Give it a good shake this time, and look into it, not at it." he added, smiling with encouragement.

She shook it very hard so bubbles rose to the top of the glass sphere. She looked again, relaxing her eyes. Her vision began to cross slightly. Her ears drooped. She wasn't looking for anything this time but just wanted to see what, if anything, she could see. She inspected the craftsmanship of the sleigh, guessed at the composition of the snow, and began to think of the elf that must have made the globe. She gently tipped the globe back and forth to keep the snow aloft. Her mind began to wander and suddenly a face emerged in the swirling snow, then another, then lots and lots of faces swirling in the globe's blizzard. Some of the faces were laughing, others crying, talking, or simply sleeping. They tumbled over and replaced each other like a kaleidoscope. They moved quickly to the front then just as quickly receded. Her face turned to a frown. She looked up at Santa.

"There are so many of them."

"Yes, but not as many as you think."

"Who are they?"

"Everyone, and no one."

Jojo frowned, "I don't understand."

Santa turned and said to Frit, "You try."

Frit flew over and landed on Jojo's left ear. The ear flinched furiously and knocked her off her perch. Un-phased she flittered down to Jojo's shoulder. Jojo shook the globe for Frit. Jojo watched Frit as she took her turn staring at the toy. Frit's eyes widened. She looked at Jojo, then they both looked at Santa.

"Now look into it at the same time."

They shrugged then both gazed into the globe while Jojo shook it for a third time. The number of faces diminished dramatically. Santa looked at Bort and tilted his head in the direction of the globe.

"You, too."

Bort scooted beside Jojo and the three of them stared deeply into the glass ball.

Quickly only a handful of faces remained.

Jojo looked up at Santa and the number of faces Frit and Bort saw grew dramatically.

"What happened?"

"Simple. The globe finds people you like when you look into the globe. So by all of you looking into the globe at the same time it shows only those individuals that all of you like."

Bort looked up, then down, testing Santa's theory and the ball. The other two watched the globe as the same faces emerged then disappeared with each of Bort's glances. After several times, Frit exclaimed, "Stop it!" Bort smiled. He quickly glanced up and down one more time just to irritate Frit. Santa and Jojo smiled while Frit's scowl deepened.

"So these are the possible hosts?"

"Yes," Santa replied. His smile diminished as he began to realize that this was the beginning of his end but the trio did not notice as they were captivated by the faces swirling in the ball.

"How are we to find them?"

Santa's smile reemerged, "Well, the reindeer do need exercise between Christmases."

The thought of actually flying in Santa's sleigh excited Jojo. This was a dream come true for anyone, especially an elf.

"When do we leave?" she asked smiling broadly.

"'We' don't," said Santa, "but you three leave tonight."

19. Take a Ride

Santa had not given them very clear instructions on what to do or where to go because he had never done this himself. His closest experience was when he had been found by similar creatures as a young boy many, many years before. His memories of the evening were faint. The images were fuzzy and disorganized. His most vivid memory was lying in his straw bed tucked under heavy wool blankets. Wind whistled through the cracks around the windows which were covered with oiled animal skins. These were used instead of glass to allow some dim light into the log cabin since his family was unable to afford glass. He was wide awake late at night with his younger brother in the loft listening very intently to the sounds as though waiting for something. Everyone else was sound asleep. He knew this because of the distinctive snoring of each of his parents. His father bellowed like a goat when he inhaled and tweeted like a tin whistle when he exhaled. His mother contributed short chattering sounds. His father claimed she also drooled which everyone but her thought was funny. Franz (that was his name before he was 'found') was staring at the hand-hewn boards supporting the thatched roof. The thatching was thick and kept the rain out but wind had a way of blowing in just enough to create an uncomfortable draft. He was trying hard to stay warm when he heard a sound below. He knew it wasn't his parents and he was sure he had put the dog outside earlier to keep the raccoons away. The wooden latch on the door popped open, then a few seconds later it shut again. He quietly rose to his elbows and peered through the rough sawn railing to the dirt floor eight feet below. He saw in the faint glow of the fire several very odd looking creatures.

What Santa was able to tell the trio was that the globe had the power to direct them where they needed to go. He knew this because his own childhood visitors told him that is what had happened. When all three looked into the globe a human would appear and the globe somehow communicated the destination to the reindeer and, voilà, off they would go. Easy as that.

"What happens when we get wherever we are going?" Jojo asked.

"You'll figure it out," Santa replied. The truth was he had no idea but he was confident the details would be sorted out at the proper time. "Along with your natural curiosity is your ability to figure things out." They stared at him, unconvinced.

Santa confidently continued, "There are two types of people in the world, those who need to be told what to do and those who can figure things out." The threesome blinked in unison waiting for the moment of enlightenment. "You three are able to figure things out."

Jojo's ears squeezed together trying to understand his meaning. The more Santa said the less sense he made. At first this adventure sounded like a fine idea but flying around to who knows where to find who knows who was getting uncomfortable.

The sleigh was about the size of a large wheel barrow and was pulled by a single reindeer. The reindeer's name was Walter. He was not very large but seemed perfectly up to the challenge. He stood patiently while Santa hooked up the harness. Normally the stable elves would have done this with much fanfare but under the circumstances Santa thought it best to keep a low profile. The sleigh looked exactly like the one in the snow globe which in turn was a miniaturized version of Santa's Christmas sleigh, painted a deep red with gold and white trim. Tassels hung from the rails. It didn't need to be any larger given that the total size of the three passengers was quite small. Santa noticed they began to stir uncomfortably as they thought about their challenge, glancing at each other and the floor, so he promptly shuffled them into the sleigh, whispered something into Walter's ear, and like a shot he jerked the sleigh into the air and off they went.

The small size of the sleigh did not diminish Jojo's excitement. She had never flown before despite imagining it all of her life. Frit didn't need to ride in the sleigh since she could fly but she perched herself on the front just to be part of the group. Jojo had expected Bort to stand on the sleigh's floor having only ever seen gnomes stand in their rigid hiding position. She was surprised to find that he was able to sit after all. His feet barely reached the edge of the short bench, looking very uncomfortable even though the velvet red seat was quite soft.

Santa waved to them as the sleigh flew away into the night sky. There were no sleigh bells because those were only used for formal occasions and would draw unnecessary attention. In the end though their attempt at stealth failed as the sight of a flying sleigh was hard to hide. Speculation began to spread through the North Pole, especially among the gnomes and their close kinsmen the trolls, who are notorious rumor mongers. However none of the rumors guessed the reason for the secret trip.

Jojo looked back nervously as the sleigh moved away from the ground. Santa leaned back slightly to watch as they flew away. When they were out of sight Santa turned and walked slowly back to the house. He was very tired. Mrs. Claus met him at the door and gently helped him inside.

The sleigh sailed into the dark sky and the clouds enveloped the team. The air was crisp with swirling snow but surprisingly they were not cold. Something about the sleigh's aerodynamics kept the cold night air away. Jojo slowly relaxed as she began to get used to the sensation of flying. Bort was less comfortable and remained rigid in his seat firmly squeezing the arm rest, eventually standing on the seat. Frit enjoyed letting someone else do the flying and stared straight ahead.

Jojo cleared her throat, "What exactly are we doing again?"

"Looking for someone we don't know in a place we've never been." Bort replied.

"Then what?" Jojo continued.

Bort continued to stare straight ahead and stated as a matter-of-fact, "We grab the captive and return him to Santa."

"The 'captive'?"

"Of course. What else would you call him?"

Jojo looked at Frit, "It doesn't sound very nice when you say it like that."

20. What's That?

After they had flown for a while twinkles of light began to appear below in the dark. At first there were only a few but the longer they flew the more frequent they became. Bundles of lights began to form then disappear quickly as Walter pulled them at an amazing speed. Jojo's eye followed them toward the horizon. Lights popped up in all different directions, scattered as far as she could see. In the distance a large yellow glow appeared. It looked at first like the setting sun, but as they came closer, the lights became more intense. The yellow light fractured into a multitude of colors.

Jojo's ears picked up the distance hum as they approached a city. They were bigger than anything she had dreamed possible. A forest of tall buildings, each full of countless rooms stacked on top, and beside other rooms. The hum grew into a loud noise. To Jojo it was deafening. Then there was the smell. Stale and sour like a rotten marshmallows and burnt cotton candy.

They descended weaving between the taller buildings. Walter seemed to know exactly where he was going. He aimed for one of the shorter buildings that was brown with steam hissing out of pipes in its roof. They landed smoothly and soon found themselves standing on a metal platform looking through a dirty window. They never imagined the variety of things they saw. There was a thick furry blanket covering the entire floor, big puffy chairs, and machines that blinked with moving pictures—the purpose of which they could only guess.

"Are we sure this is the right place?" Frit asked.

"According to the globe, it is," Jojo answered.

"How should we grab it?" Bort asked earnestly.

Jojo pushed her nose against the glass to get a better look. A boy was sitting on the largest puffy chair drawing pictures on scraps of paper: the first human she had ever seen other than Santa. The boy must be a child because he was nowhere near Santa's size yet the similarities were unmistakable. Jojo could see he was drawing a picture of a house with smoke coming from its chimney. The boy paused and looked up. He glanced around the room sensing something out of the ordinary. His eyes rested on the window through which Jojo was looking. The boy walked slowly toward them holding a crayon in one hand and his picture dangling from the other. As he approached a small dog bounded into the room, ran past the boy nearly knocking him down and jumped at the window. Jojo jolted backward, Frit flew straight up, and Bort stood as rigid as a post. The dog hit the glass so hard they all thought the window would surely break. The dog yapped with a loud, piercing, insistent bark. He jumped straight up in the air as he barked, scrapping his nails on the window sill creating a fearsome racket. A tall man came running into the room yelling at the dog to stop. Being a typical house pet the dog ignored the command and continued to yap focusing solely on the intruders he had discovered. The man's attention turned to why the dog was barking. He cautiously walked over to the window and looked out.

"What's out there, Maxie? What do you see?"

The dog grew even more excited, his instincts to attack taking over now that he was joined by a member of his pack.

"It's a funny looking kid." the boy told the man.

The father looked over his shoulder to the boy then back through the window. He approached closer, very slowly. Inch by inch his nose moved to the window. He and Jojo were now separated by only a quarter-inch of glass.

"Do you see him?" the boy asked.

The man looked a few more seconds then stood up straight and turned around, his back to the window.

"There's nothing out there."

The boy pointed toward the window, "But he's right there."

"I'm sorry honey but there's nothing there."

From another room, a woman's voice called out, "What's going on?"

The man yelled back, "It's nothing. Max is just making a fuss again. Probably a siren."

"But he is right there! I can see him!" insisted the boy.

The man looked back to the window, rubbed the frost from the glass and looked out again. The threesome remained motionless and stared back at the man. The man opened the window and stuck his head out. The dog's barking became louder and more persistent. The man looked to the left, the right, up, down and pulled himself back into the room shutting the window to keep out the cold.

"Max, settle down!" He instructed the dog, then looked to the boy, "There's nothing out there dear other than a dirty old doll someone left on the fire escape. Go back to your drawing." And with that the man picked up the growling dog under one arm, walked over and gave the little boy a kiss on the head and headed into the other room, the dog frantically trying to wiggle away and return to the hunt but the man held him tight.

"It's nothing," the man said to the unseen woman as he entered the other room.

The three friends looked at each other utterly surprised. The man couldn't see Jojo, didn't notice Frit, and thought Bort was a 'dirty old doll,' but the little boy and the dog saw them.

"I don't like this place," Bort announced. Before he even finished his statement Frit had already turned and was flying back to the sled on the roof. Jojo paused and looked back.

The boy looked sad and waved goodbye. Jojo waved back, turned, and followed her friends up the fire escape.

21. Disappointment

Many hours later they returned to the North Pole having made several more stops, each similar to the first. They were barked at, hissed at, cried at, screamed at, yelled at and run away from. In all cases the child for whom they searched could see the trio, as could the animals and the other young children, but none of the older humans could except for someone occasionally mistaking Bort for a doll or statue.

They felt discouraged thinking this was going to be an easy task or at least a quick one. They had expected to be welcomed with bright smiling faces and eager participation. Who wouldn't want to be Santa Claus, after all? The reality was quite the opposite. They sat by Santa's fireplace recounting the disastrous results waiting for Santa. They had no doubt he would also be disappointed with their result. They hoped he would have some suggestions for the next outing as they clearly felt they had no idea how to complete their task.

Mrs. Claus entered the room. She jumped startled by their presence, clutching her hands in front of her chest. She then surveyed the room anxiously.

"Where is the new guest?"

"We couldn't find one."

Mrs. Claus' eyes widened, she repeated, "Couldn't find one?"

They each shook their heads no.

Jojo clarified hopefully, "We saw several though."

"But we couldn't catch any of them," Bort added.

"Do you think Santa could provide some more suggestions?" ask Frit.

Mrs. Claus sank into the rocking chair and stared gloomily at the fire. They did not know what to say. This was the reaction they feared. Not only had they let Santa down they had disappointed Mrs. Claus as well. But she offered no complaint nor did she try to make them feel better with 'That's all right.' She simply sat in her chair.

"Where is Santa?" Jojo asked.

"He's in bed. He's not... feeling particularly well."

"Is he okay?"

Mrs. Claus hesitated then replied gloomily, "No. I'm afraid not."

"Did something happen to him?"

"Time." Mrs. Claus replied with a forced smile. "He's very old and simply worn down."

They did not know what to say so they stood in silence waiting for Mrs. Claus to continue.

She sat up a little straighter and looked at them with a sense of urgency. "You have very little time left. What you have been tasked to do is extremely hard and more important than you know. Even more important is that you must do it quickly. If you cannot find the next Santa host soon this..." she looked about the room, "...will all be gone."

'Gone?' The three friends were stunned. The magnitude of their task slowly settled in.

Before they could ask any questions Mrs. Claus explained, "The Santa spirit provides a sort of magic that enables all of this to exist. The Spirit creates good will among all the creatures that live here who would otherwise not associate with each other. Their cooperation built this place and allows the Spirit's work to continue. So, if the Spirit has no host, it will leave and everything around you will eventually disappear."

"What will happen then?"

"Everyone will go back to their forests, caves, or ponds," She smiled gently at Bort, "and front yards."

The sense of dread began to sweep over them.

"Does everyone else here know what is going on?" Frit ventured.

"No. Some suspect, others are making up their own stories but no one knows for sure and it needs to stay that way. The Santa spirit is the stabilizing foundation. Uncertainty would spread like a box of dropped marbles and have the same effect as if the Santa spirit had already left. There is a delicate balance that must be maintained."

"What do we do now?"

"Exactly what you set out to do earlier tonight, but you need to do it quickly. Very quickly, I fear."

22. All Alone

Erin was a young girl. She was twelve years old and used to have a normal family as far as she could tell. No one yelled much or acted crazy except her fifteen-year-old brother who was beginning to show an interest in girls, which Erin thought was kind of yucky. She didn't think about boys much. The main boy she interacted with was her father who read the newspaper every day before he dropped her off at school. Her mother was constantly on the move running errands, cleaning the house, and working on projects until she wore herself out and collapsed in front of the television at the end of each day.

Erin secretly believed in Santa. She wanted him to be real. But her family had not made it easy. Whenever she raised the possibility her brother called her dumb and her mother called her silly. Her father didn't seem to have an opinion one way or the other but never actually discouraged the belief. He hadn't encourage it either. All he ever said was, "We may never know."

But that seemed like a long time ago. She looked out of the window from behind the couch that had become her new private spot. She played quietly so as not to disturb Aunt Clara with whom she now lived.

No one had explained to her what had happened in a way she could comprehend. Aunt Clara referred to it as the 'accident.' The court room also used the word 'accident' along with a lot of other words that didn't make sense to a twelve year old. But what she did know was that her family had died and she would never see them again.

It all happened very suddenly. She had been at home alone with the teenaged babysitter, even though Erin strongly believed she was too old to need anyone to stay with her much less a 'babysitter'. When the phone rang Erin ran to answer it but she didn't recognize the number on the caller ID so she let the sitter answer it instead. The sitter held the phone to her ear. She listened for a second or two then her free hand rushed to cover her mouth. The sitter began to shake and her face turned white. She dropped the phone and kneeled down to give Erin a smothering hug. It was hard to breathe and started to hurt.

A short time later Aunt Clara showed up at Erin's house with two police officers. Erin asked where her parents were and everyone looked away like she had said something bad. The sitter turned quickly and left the room crying. The police officers seemed to be inspecting the tops of their shoes as they slowly moved away looking very uncomfortable. Erin looked to her aunt, someone she only saw on special occasions and even then never talked to her. Erin didn't think her aunt liked kids. Erin supposed it wasn't a coincidence that her aunt never had any children of her own.

Aunt Clara replied more emotionally than she expected, "They're gone, dear."

Erin knew they were gone, that's why the babysitter had been here. "But when are they coming home?"

Unsure how to console a small person Aunt Clara simply replied "They're not."

Erin did not react. Her mind was swimming with possibilities of what happened. Had they been arrested? Did they get lost? Were they in trouble? Was she in trouble? Nothing made sense.

Soon after Erin moved in with Aunt Clara and in a few short weeks they had settled into a routine of sorts. It consisted of Aunt Clara reading gossip magazines and Erin staying quietly out of the way. They ate microwave dinners. At home Erin would have watched television but Aunt Clara did not have a TV, at least not one that worked. Aunt Clara's only generated a screen of white snow and crackling static sounds. She blamed it on the 'Feds' for allowing only digital signals, which the rabbit ears on her TV could not decipher. But neither Erin nor Aunt Clara seemed to miss it. Occasionally Erin would turn it on when her aunt wasn't home just to check to see if anything had appeared. She didn't like the hissing noise so she would turn the volume all the way off and just stare at the white static looking for patterns. She would day dream and forget her loneliness. There was something peaceful about the patterns that emerged and disappeared amidst the white squall. She imagined she could see her parents or brother looking back at her but knew that couldn't be true. As soon as she heard Aunt Clara climb the stairs to the front door Erin would quickly turn off the television so as not disturb her aunt or give her aunt the idea that Erin was going crazy. Maybe crazy wouldn't be such a bad thing...

Aunt Clara was not a bad person. She did not beat Erin or even scold her. In fact they barely spoke to each other. Aunt Clara lacked any sense of purpose, energy or emotions. She seemed to merely exist. Aunt Clara had been a checkout clerk for nearly forty years at Sammy's Supermart grocery store. She had never married and, as far as Erin could tell, had no friends. Erin's family never visited her aunt's house when her parents were still alive even though they were each other's only remaining relatives. Aunt Clara would periodically come to Erin's house for holidays but never stayed long.

Aunt Clara didn't like people. After forty, years of complaints, idle chatter and endless speculation about the weather she had decided people were uninteresting. She had liked boys at one point a long, long time ago, but they did not show any interest in her so she quit trying to get noticed. Afterwards her life became much simpler. She received her weekly paycheck which grew every few years when the Government forced Sammy's management to increase the minimum wage.

She also learned that at the end of each month when the magazines were replaced with the newer issue the old ones would be deposited in the trash bins behind the store which she referred to as the 'dumpster library.' Aunt Clara made sure she worked late those days in order to make a 'withdrawal' after everyone else had gone home. She would read the articles behind the glossy pictures that had stared at her every day in the preceding month from the racks that lined the checkout aisle. She finally found out what the popular people said, what they did, and what everyone else said about them. She didn't care about the latest miracle diet, or top ten ways to find a man, or make the man you had happy. Instead she absorbed the tales of extravagant lives, the descriptions of the places far away where every desire came true. It reminded her of the dreams and aspirations she had back when life seemed to matter. She was simply making the best of the life she had as her clock slowly wound down to zero.

Erin reminded Aunt Clara of herself, but not in an expected way. Erin reminded her that her life was littered with crushed dreams. She couldn't blame the girl. Having her entire family killed in a car crash by a teenage driver distracted by a text message was a hard wound from which to recover. She, like Erin, was simply making it through one day at a time, and if possible, contentedly. Unfortunately for both Erin and Aunt Clara, Aunt Clara had lost the ability to communicate, and Erin had only just begun to learn. They settled into their own private, parallel lives in the same house where they simply existed. Both wishing for a better future.

23. Curious

The last rays of sun skimmed over the tree tops and shone into the glass window illuminating the narrow space behind the couch Erin now thought of as her own. Aunt Clara was sitting at the kitchen table flipping through the small stack of magazines recovered the night before. Erin had no toys of which to speak. Barbies had consumed her life before but they held no interest for her now. Nothing from her previous life seemed particularly important and when she found something that reminded her of those days it made her very sad. Instead she had in a sense started over. She took Aunt Clara's magazines after her aunt was done with them and cut out interesting looking faces, rolled them around her finger tips and secured them with tape to create finger puppets. She spent hours behind the couch having quiet conversations about... everything.

She watched the last rays of the sun reflect off the glass thinking it was almost dinner time. She saw the neighbor's cat. He was right on time. As far as she could tell he never missed a meal because he was so big. This time though, rather than lying on top of the metal trash can lid waiting for supper as he typically did, he was on his tip toes, back arched, fur standing on end, tail straight up, and hissing. Erin rolled to her knees to get a better look. At first she didn't see anything but as her eyes adjusted to the sunset's glare there it was in the middle of the yard. 'Where did that come from?' she wondered to herself. A little toy. A bearded man with a pointed red hat, black boots, and a black belt around his pot belly. The back yard was fenced all the way around so no one would have been able to put it there without some effort.

"How did you get here?" she said out loud to herself.

She scanned the rest of the yard for signs of anything else un-usual but there were none. She hopped up and headed out the back door for a closer look.

"Where are you going?" Aunt Clara asked, more as a reaction than an honest question.

"Out back for a second."

Aunt Clara turned a page and replied without looking up, "Don't be long. We'll be eating soon."

That was the last thing Aunt Clara would ever say to Erin.

24. New Friends

Erin pulled the door shut behind her. The sun light was sinking quickly. She walked to the spot where the doll had been but it had disappeared. The cat still stood on the trash can. He noticed Erin and leapt to the top of the fence and was gone. Erin's eyes scoured the yard. She knew she had seen the toy. She was sure of it. She took a couple steps and turned around to change her perspective. She saw it beside the fence. What a strange thing, it was in the middle of the small yard a second ago, or so she thought, now it was at the edge of the yard instead.

"That's weird," she commented aloud to herself.

She walked toward it for a better look fully intent on picking it up. Just then a huge bug flew at her face. Her head jerked back instinctively and swatted at it. It flew back several feet from her head and hovered at eye level.

"Did you just try to hit me?" it said in a high-pitched squeak.

Erin's mouth dropped open. The little flying creature slowly moved toward her. Erin was dumbstruck and couldn't move.

"You do know it's not polite to hit don't you?"

The bug pivoted in the air and faced the back of the house.

"I'm not so sure this one is right. Do you?" Frit asked Jojo.

Erin followed the fairy's gaze to the trash can and saw a terribly thin little girl with pointy ears and hands resting on her hips.

Jojo replied, "Well what did you expect? You almost put her eye out!"

Erin was speechless.

"Wasn't I was just trying to get her attention?" Frit retorted.

Jojo shook her head and took a step forward speaking to Erin, "I have to apologize for my friend. Fairies are sometimes hard to understand if you know what I mean."

"I certainly don't know what you mean," Frit replied.

"A-hah! That wasn't a question! You didn't ask a question!" Jojo exclaimed.

"Didn't I?"

"Ahem!" A deep voice coughed from the ground behind Erin. "Would you two please stop bickering and hurry up?"

Erin looked over her shoulder and only saw the doll, now a mere two feet away. She blinked twice then asked, "Did you say that?"

Bort stood perfectly still, exhibiting the best hidden form he could muster.

"Yes he did," Jojo replied. "He doesn't say much but he is correct. We need to hurry."

Jojo took a step closer to Erin. "We desperately need your help."

Erin tried to regain her composure, then looking at each of the creatures in turn, "Who are you?", "What are you?", "Why do you need my help?"

Frit landed on Jojo's shoulder and noted in response to Erin's questions, "I at least like the way she talks, don't you?"

Jojo tried her best to quickly summarize the situation. Frit added some unnecessary rhetorical questions which caused more confusion than help. Bort tried to fill in bits of information he thought necessary to give the full picture (he was a good story teller after all, once he decided to talk). Jojo though, being very efficient, quickly caught Erin up on the whole situation clarifying that Frit was not a bug, Bort was indeed a gnome, and she was definitely an elf.

By now Erin was sitting on the bottom stair step listening to the remarkable story. She had not heard stories like this since before the accident. Her mother was a fabulous story teller and would create new stories every night before bed until Erin turned eleven. On her birthday, Erin decided stories were for babies and simply said good night to her mother who was in the kitchen cleaning up from Erin's birthday party. She put herself to bed the way big girls do and turned off her bedroom light. She lay there with her back to the door and eyes open for the longest time expecting her mother to tuck her in, hoping she wouldn't, but wishing she would. Her mother in the meantime sat at the kitchen table, alone realizing her little girl was growing up and needed some space. After Erin fell asleep her mother sneaked into Erin's room and kissed her good night. Erin felt the kiss in her dreams and smiled.

"Will you help us?" Jojo asked.

Erin raised her eyes. Even sitting Erin was taller than the elf standing. She thought for a few moments digesting everything she had just been told. She liked the story but she was old enough now to know fact from fiction.

At last Erin announced in a most confident tone, "I don't believe you".

Jojo sat on the ground with a thud. This was not the answer she expected. Erin was the first visit in which the trio had actually made any meaningful contact. Besides, didn't Erin know that elves can't lie?

"I don't believe in Santa," Erin continued. "That's for babies. I also don't believe in you. I must admit you seem real enough but I'm sure this can't be happening. Gnomes, elves, fairies, the North Pole—all of it is just make believe." She looked at each of them trying to remember every detail for when she woke up. It would make a good game behind the couch. She added for clarity, "It's just a dream, nothing more."

Frit and Jojo exchanged glances not really sure what to do next. Then in the blink of an eye Bort appeared next to Erin's leg and kicked her in the shin. The pain shot up her leg so quickly she couldn't even scream. Her mouth flew open trying to catch her breath as she grasped her leg tightly. Jojo and Frit were too shocked to react.

"Do you still think it's a dream?" Bort asked angrily.

In the end, the decision was not difficult. Erin agreed to go with them, because, well... why not? She fully expected that this was all still a very pleasant dream that she did not want to end.

The initial pull of the sleigh was very realistic and the breeze in her face added to the sensation. But as time wore on the dizzying height and small distant lights below began to make what was happening all too real. She was flying in a sleigh with creatures she had only just met. She could only imagine the trouble she would be in when she returned to Aunt Clara's house late for dinner.

25. Without a Trace

The police were notified an hour after Aunt Clara looked up from last month's "Hollywood Tattler." She had become entranced by the story of a starlet's island home. It dawned on her they had not eaten dinner and that Erin was quieter than usual. Had Erin actually come back in? Aunt Clara wasn't sure. She called Erin's name and did a cursory search of the house, especially behind the couch. She looked out the back door into the fenced yard. Darkness had settled in so she had to turn on the back door light. She called Erin's name but there was no answer. She turned around did a more thorough search. As she looked she talked to herself. She began talking to herself regularly over the past 30 years and these conversations had grown in frequency and intensity as her isolation grew. "I am going to have a long talk that kid when I find her. Does she have any idea how inconvenient this is? I never asked for this responsibility. Serve's her right if she went and got herself lost." As she continued her search though she became worried. As much as Aunt Clara cherished her independence and lack of responsibility for anyone other than herself, she had come to enjoy the presence of another person, even if that person was still a child. She went outside and screamed Erin's name with no luck. By the time she called the police she was in a full panic. Her mind raced with foul possibilities. Who would have taken her? Why would anyone take her? Did she run away? Was I that hard to live with? The real answer never even remotely entered her mind.

Erin would have been surprised to learn that her picture was placed on the front page of the local paper, then the missing children web sites, then the national news as no clues whatsoever were discovered. The stories of her family's misfortune and apparent lack of supervision by her aunt made it too juicy for the news media to ignore. Aunt Clara, in turn, was featured on the front page of the tabloids she had previously prized for reasons very different from those she had dreamed. She was swiftly convicted in the court of public opinion for neglect but never was charged with any misdeeds by the local authorities due to lack of evidence. No one had paid attention to the finger puppet left in the middle of the back yard nor to the two skid tracks left by a miniature sleigh just beyond the fence line. Aunt Clara never touched a tabloid magazine again.

26. Who Is This?

When Erin's feet touched the ground again she was feeling light-headed. She had not eaten in quite a while, was still shaky from the flight and disoriented by the brightly lit surroundings of the North Pole. Everything appeared in miniature except for a large gingerbread house which closely resembled the one in the Hansel and Gretel story her father used to read to her. She was pretty sure there was no witch present, or at least she hoped not. She was ushered into Santa's study and given a warm glass of milk. Considering diets of Jojo, Bort and Frit consisted exclusively of candy, bugs, and light, her new friends had no reason to believe humans would want anything else. Needless to say the dinner was not what Erin had in mind but she did find a plate of cookies by the fireplace that was very good indeed.

Mrs. Claus entered the room shortly after their return. She stopped abruptly in the doorway. Her eyes fixed on Erin. The trio had relaxed and smiled, lounging about the cozy room knowing they had accomplished their task. Erin in turn stared back at Mrs. Claus. She looked nothing like Erin had imagined, but upon seeing her, Mrs. Claus looked exactly as she should.

"And who is this?" Mrs. Claus asked in a very motherly tone. Mrs. Claus had been exceedingly happy these many years with her husband but had always had a void she could never fill. She had wished she could have been a mother. She tried to fill the emptiness by mothering Santa, the reindeer, and the creatures she encountered, but it was not the same. Seeing Erin here now was about as close as she would ever come, and just in time.

"This is Erin," Jojo spoke up.

Mrs. Claus considered Erin for minute then stated the obvious. "She's a girl."

Silence.

"Why did you choose a girl?"

Silence.

Jojo rose sheepishly, "We weren't told to choose anyone in particular."

"But she's a girl." Mrs. Claus repeated.

The issue slowly dawned on the trio why this might be an issue. Santa had never been anything but a boy as far as any of them knew. The fact they had found someone at all who was willing to come with them blinded them to this seemingly obvious detail. They looked in stunned silence at Erin not knowing what to do next.

"Please stand up, my dear," Mrs. Claus directed Erin.

Erin was still not sure what was going on or understood her role as she was simply riding a wave in a sea of strange events. She rose from the chair and looked up at Mrs. Claus.

"How old are you?"

"Twelve."

"Do you have any family? Parents? Brothers or sisters?"

Erin paused. This was the first time she had been asked this. She answered quietly, "Not anymore". This was also the first time she had acknowledged it to anyone, even herself. Her eyes began to well with tears as she felt suddenly alone.

Mrs. Claus slowly circled Erin looking her over. She stopped in front of her, knelt down, put her hands on Erin's shoulders and looked Erin in the eye. Whispering to no one, Mrs. Claus said, "She's perfect."

The trio were utterly confused at this point. The exhilaration of finding the next Santa was replaced by the realization they had completely missed the mark by bringing back a girl, who now happened to be "perfect." Erin had no idea what was going on or how to react. That left only Mrs. Claus with any sense of what was to come.

Mrs. Claus noticed the lack of comprehension and stunned silence on each of their faces. She smiled, sat in the rocker, leaned toward Erin and said, "My name, before becoming Mrs. Claus, was Marie."

27. Wandering

Marie was 14 years old and lived in a heavily wooded area of Eastern Europe. She was the third of seven children. Her parents were very loving and supportive but were also worried about her adventurous spirit. There was nothing feminine or ladylike about Marie. There were chores to be done, rules by which to abide and expectations to live up to. Marie ignored them all. The plans for her wedding were already being set. All that was missing was a groom. So far, the dowry they had collected included three chickens, two ducks, a biscuit bowl, and a half-finished comforter—not too bad considering how desperately poor they were. However their expectations were not high, so any boy with anything to offer would be seriously considered. Marie, for her part, would much rather chase rabbits and climb trees than learn how to knit or cook, much less take care of a husband and the expected brood of children that would follow. She often roamed through the woods despite warnings of wolves, bears and witches.

One warm spring day as dusk began to settle in she set out to wander through the woods looking for excitement. Her chores were done after much effort on her part, her mother was busy with her younger siblings and her father was sowing the last rows of oats in the field. She turned her back on the little farm confident that something new to discover would surely present itself if she looked long enough. On this day it found her instead.

She was following the tracks of a wild animal. She was pretty sure it was from a deer but the hove marks were unusually small. Then there appeared two straight parallel lines on either side of the narrow trail. She had seen similar markings in the winter when they used a sled to pull firewood from the forest. Her curiosity peaked and she sped up slightly. The marks led around the corner of a large boulder. There before her stood a large hairy woman with a grossly misshaped head, a short bearded man in a green suit with a tall black hat, and a little ugly creature that looked like a potato with arms and legs. She would soon learn they were a troll, a leprechaun and a goblin. They looked at each other for a few minutes. Marie felt no fear and soon learned they too had set out on an adventure. They had been sent on a mission to find her. Marie sat against the boulder as they explained their situation and how they came to find her through the use of a magical ball. It led them to this spot, and here she was.

Marie did not need much convincing. An adventure to someplace magical was in fact a dream come true—anything to take her away from the life that had been planned for her. This unforeseen meeting was more than she could have hoped. She did not like having to leave home so abruptly without telling her mother where she was going but that was only a passing concern. She thought her parents already had their hands full with her six brothers and sisters and would probably appreciate one less mouth to feed. In fact, she felt like the forgotten child. Everyone was too busy to be interested in her. She assumed she would see them again within a day or two. She was wrong. She would never see her home again.

Marie climbed into a small red sleigh pulled by two reindeer. The size of the troll after all required more deer power. She eagerly awaited what was to come next.

The search for her lasted many days and the hope for her return lasted many weeks, but in those parts when someone disappeared they were gone for good. Her family grieved for their loss because Marie's adventurous spirit was an inspiration, reminding them of the possibilities that existed. The first Christmas following her disappearance, and every Christmas after, a present for each of her family members miraculously arrived at their small house in the woods with a note simply signed 'M'. They couldn't explain how the gifts arrived or who delivered them but believed in their hearts Marie was okay.

28. Getting Tired

When Mrs. Claus finished her brief story the only part that became clear was that Mrs. Claus had at one time been someone else. What this didn't tell them was what would happen next.

The office door opened. A dwarf stood in the doorway, looked at Mrs. Claus and simply shook his head. Mrs. Claus' face turned grim. She immediately stood up and instructed, "Please follow me."

She led them down a short hallway to another room. She gently opened the door and they filed in behind her. They found Santa lying in bed, seemingly asleep. His breathing was shallow and slightly labored causing all of them concern. The door squeaked lightly as Erin shut it behind her, being the last to enter the room. Santa's eyes cracked opened. He turned his head in the direction of the noise and smiled to find his wife and new found friends. He had a hopeful and expectant look on his face.

"Well?"

Mrs. Claus replied, "They found a girl."

His eyes widened and he raised his head slightly, "Marvelous! That is good news. Very good news." He then sank back into the fluffy white pillow that cradled his head and shut his eyes to gather his energy.

Mrs. Claus ran her fingers through Santa's hair, trying in a small way to make him more comfortable. She looked at him and added very gently, "She is exactly who we hoped for."

He nodded slightly. His energy had faded since Jojo had last seen him.

He reopened his eyes and tried to scan the room. "Where is she?" he asked.

Mrs. Claus reached around and put a hand in the middle of Erin's back and gently pushed her forward into Santa's line of sight.

"This is Erin. Erin, this is Santa." Santa smiled broadly but was clearly tired. Erin couldn't help but smile back.

"You really are real?" Erin blurted out.

He replied with a weak "Ho, Ho,..." and then coughed slightly. "I should have guessed it was Erin. It has been several years since I saw you last. You certainly have grown."

Erin's eyes narrowed, "How did you know my name? I've never seen you before."

"Of course not, you were asleep."

"So you really did eat the cookies I left by the fireplace?"

"Of course I did. I love cookies. Who else would it have been?"

"I thought my brother was playing a   trick on me."

"But you left them out all the same   didn't you?"

"Yes, just in case you were real."

"And I appreciated it very much. Thank you."

Mrs. Claus interrupted, "I'm sorry but we still have a lot to do. You get some rest Santa and we'll get back to work."

Mrs. Claus bent over and gave Santa a kiss on the forehead. He closed his eyes and almost immediately began to sleep. She took Erin's shoulders and turned her toward the door, held her arms wide and herded everyone out.

29. The List

Back in Santa's office Mrs. Claus sat in the rocking chair and stared at the floor. She appeared very tired and older than before. Her mind seemed to have wandered far away. The others stood by waiting anxiously for what to do next.

"Mrs. Claus?" Jojo started.

Mrs. Claus looked up seemingly distracted by other thoughts, "Yes, Jojo?"

"What do we do now?"

Mrs. Claus let the question register for a few seconds. Her head seemed to clear and she replied, "Show Erin the book." Mrs. Claus looked in the direction of the desk. "She'll know what to do."

Jojo, Frit and Bort looked at Erin.

Erin, slow to recognize that Mrs. Claus was referring to her, replied, "Me?"

Mrs. Claus distantly replied, "Yes dear, you."

Jojo took Erin by the hand and guided her to the desk. There was a massive book on it in front of the desk chair. Erin hesitated then pushed the chair back and stood over the book in order to read it. On the cover in large, gold, ornate lettering was written

Naughty or Nice

Erin didn't notice that Frit had flown over and landed on her shoulder to see the book better. Erin looked up from the book to Mrs. Claus. She started to ask what she was expected to do, but Mrs. Claus was staring deeply into the smoldering fire. Mrs. Claus had said Erin would know what to do but Erin had no clue. She inspected the heavy, worn book. The cover was thick brown leather intricately decorated with silver markings that seemed to glow. The unevenly cut pages had gold trim on the edges.

She opened the book to the first page. The text looked hand-written in a very neat calligraphy font. A simple a list of names in alphabetical order, last name first. Erin, not knowing what else to do began to read the names. The first was "Aaronson, Aaron Alan". There was nothing particularly interesting about the list other than each name had a little notation beside it, "Naughty" or "Nice." Erin looked over to Jojo and Bort, "It's just a list of names."

Jojo shrugged. Erin looked to Mrs. Claus who was hopelessly withdrawn.

Erin looked back at the book and read each name in turn. At first She tried to do this as rapidly as she could (it was a big book after all), but then slowed down as each of the names seemed to come alive as she read them. She began to see in her own mind a complete image of each person behind each name, what they were like and what they liked to do. She drew an immediate impression of the child, which confirmed their Naughty or Nice designation. Frit was also reading the list but only saw black ink on a slightly yellowed piece of paper.

Jojo and Bort noticed that the book began to emanate a light onto Erin's face. They took a couple steps closer. Frit saw their movement and shrugged. From Frit's perch on Erin's shoulder, Frit could see nothing unusual happening.

Erin began to pick up her reading pace turning the pages faster and faster. The trio watched Erin closely. She figured out she was able to absorb the information behind each name immediately. Instead of reading the names she began to simply scan the pages, turning them as fast as she could. Some names even began to glow more brightly than others.

"What do you see?" Jojo asked finally.

Erin ignored the question but simply replied, "It's not fast enough. I can't read them all."

Mrs. Claus uttered, "Let go of the pages."

Erin paused and they all turned to look at Mrs. Claus. She was still staring at the fire.

"What am I looking for?" Erin asked.

Mrs. Claus answered distantly, "You'll know it when you see it, just let go of the pages."

Erin withdrew her hands from the book and simply stared at the page in front of her. She didn't read the names anymore but focused on the images she saw. They began to fill her mind. When all the images from the open page was completed the page turned itself. As this continued Erin began to concentrate harder in order to absorb the information flooding into her mind. Faster and faster the pages started to turn. It now looked like a strong breeze blew across the book making the pages flip on their own.

The trio was mesmerized by the sight. Although they were accustomed to magical acts and took them as routine, they had never seen anything like this before. Erin's eyes were now closed and not even looking at the pages. The pages spun at a dizzying pace.

The breeze from the churning pages blew the hair back from her face. Then suddenly her hand slammed down on the book. Startled, Frit flew from Erin's shoulder. Erin lifted her hand, looking under her palm as if to find a bug she had just squashed. Her eyebrows furrowed slightly. She turned a couple pages forward, then several pages back until she found the name that she was looking for. She read the name to herself. Then she read out loud, "Flipper, James Sydney." She closed her eyes again and placed her hand on the writing seeming to feel the name. "Jimmy Flipper." She opened her eyes, looked at the trio, "It's Jimmy Flipper."

Mrs. Claus looked up from her stupor and repeated the name with a smile, "Jimmy Flipper."

30. Leftovers

Jimmy lay on his bed thinking about his day at school. It included reading, writing, taunts, jeers, humiliations and embarrassments. He was not the only kid teased in school, but it certainly felt like it. The brunt of most of the jokes centered on his name, it always had. Jimmy was tall and skinny making him an easy target for the football players to pick on. They would stop him in the school's hallway and say to each other, "Let's flipper him," then toss him over their shoulders. Jimmy had become so used to this he could almost land on his feet... almost. If he resisted too much they would laugh even harder and tell him, "Don't flipper-out, dude!" The fact he had overly large feet only made matters worse with the obvious insults, "Are those feet or flippers in your shoes?" He was a very good swimmer, but being on the swim team was not an option. He remembered being horrified to discover a popular TV show that featured a dolphin with his last name. It would simply be one more thing about which to be teased. Thankfully it had been discontinued many years before his time.

'Jimmy Flipper', a name more fitting for a children's bedtime story than one given to a son. Jimmy resented his ancestor who, hundreds of years before, had misspelled the original family name of 'Filipper' on some official long lost document. So here he was, the youngest in a long line of Flippers to bear the burden of a typo. There was some comfort in knowing his father too had inherited the name and that his parents had the sense not to name him "Flip" or "Chipper." All in all, "Jimmy" probably was not that bad but it didn't make the teasing any less painful, especially for a fifteen-year-old boy in high school.

He had no idea his name would draw such attention until his first day of school. When Scott Schmidlick heard Jimmy's last name during roll call he laughed out loud making Jimmy cry. In hindsight Jimmy was sure Scott was simply trying to deflect attention from his own name, and since Jimmy's name came first in the alphabetical roll call, Scott got the jump on him. This made the other boys laugh and point. The girls giggled and whispered to each other while glancing in his direction. Jimmy's tears burned on his cheeks but he couldn't stop. He rushed Scott and punched him in the stomach. The only thing the teacher saw was Scott doubled over with his arms wrapped around his belly howling. Jimmy was immediately escorted to the principal's office where he received a stern warning about misbehaving and fights. His father was required to pick him up just an hour into his formal education.

Despite repeated demands Jimmy never told the principal or his father why he punched Scott. Jimmy vowed to himself at that moment he would never cry at school again thus stripping his tormentors of some of their pleasure.

"Jimmy!" his father called from downstairs. His dad had always been something of a worry wart. He rarely left the house, working from home for a large technology company. He did all the cooking, cleaning, shopping and parenting for Jimmy, his only child. He started down the single parent path when Jimmy's mother suddenly left. It had been nine years since she went to the shopping mall to "grab a couple of things" and never returned. It also happened to be the same week Jimmy was sent home for fighting. His dad found the note she left. Written in pencil and left in the bathroom to be found later. It was brief and to the point, "I have to leave. You know why. I love you both." The 'you know why' part was what Jimmy could not forget nor understand because, in fact, he didn't understand. He asked his dad if her leaving was his fault because he had been sent home. At first his dad tried to reassure Jimmy it wasn't, but Jimmy was not convinced. He asked his dad every night when he was tucked into bed if his mom was coming home. His dad would say "I sure hope so." Then his dad would start to cry. Even at six years old Jimmy realized his need to know the truth was not as painful as the answer his dad wouldn't share.

It seemed secrets ran in the Flipper family along with the name. He loved his dad tremendously but as a teenager Jimmy felt a growing need to exert his own independence. Maybe it was the prospect of finally getting out of the prison his school had become, or maybe he was still mad for not having his mom around. In either case he found he was distancing himself from his father, ready for the next chapter in his life.

"Up here, Dad." Jimmy replied in a monotone, disinterested, teenager voice. His father knew he worried too much about Jimmy but he was glad his son had so many good friends at school. Jimmy seemed to be pretty popular with the other guys. He had heard them shout to him as he got off the bus calling, "See you on the flipper side!" He imagined Jimmy would also be getting interested in girls soon.

Girls. It did not seem that long ago when he had met Jimmy's mother. They were high school sweethearts. They were inseparable and married a month after graduation despite their parents urging them to wait until after college. Their parents wanted them to actually date other people! But they loved one another...at least they did for a while. Jimmy was born in time for their one-year high school reunion. By the time they reached their five-year reunion Jimmy's mother had become distant, angry and depressed. During one particularly loud fight she blurted out, "This was all a big mistake. All of it! You. Marriage. Jimmy. I should have listened to my parents." She realized what she had said as soon as she said it. She ran and locked herself in their bedroom until the next morning. When she finally came out she mumbled, "I have to grab a couple things from the store," and that was the last he saw of her.

Fortunately Jimmy had been asleep during the fight but his father never answered Jimmy's question 'Why?' He could never put Jimmy in the position of thinking it was somehow Jimmy's fault. Besides, Jimmy never asked about her anymore so perhaps in the best of all worlds his son had forgotten about her. "Good riddance!" he said out loud now to himself. But in his heart he still missed her as much as the day she left.

"Good riddance to what?" Jimmy asked confused by the outburst.

Jimmy's dad jumped. He had been standing at the sink washing dishes. Jimmy had made his way down the stairs unnoticed. He looked at Jimmy then back to the sink, "Uh, the last of the lasagna that I ruined three days ago. I threw it out."

"Thank goodness. That was pretty bad."

Jimmy's father's eye brows furrowed slightly and replied, "I actually kind of liked it."

"Come on Dad," Jimmy countered. "Soy lasagna with wheat germ noodles and plantains! What were you thinking?"

"When you say it like that... I'm not sure." He turned back to the dishes. "How was school today?"

"The usual."

"Learn anything?"

"If you consider Pythagorean's Theorem as 'learning anything', then yes, but what good is it?"

"Hey, come on. That's important stuff!"

Jimmy gave him a dubious stare.

"You can't build a house without knowing that," Jimmy's father said confidently.

"Right," Jimmy agreed disinterestedly. He changed the subject to something much more important, "So, what's for dinner?"

"Have I got a surprise for you?"

"Let me guess, a T-bone steak, mashed potatoes with gravy, French fries and macaroni and cheese."

"One cow and three starches? I don't think so," his father replied feigning disgust.

"Okay then, tofu burgers on whole wheat buns with soy cheese and Brussels sprouts," Jimmy said sullenly.

"How did you guess?"

"It's what we have for dinner every Thursday."

31. Glimmer of Hope

Santa slept uneasily. He dreamt of that night many, many years before when he looked over the edge of the loft to find strangers in his home. In his dream the room was filled with of dozens of creatures he had never before seen. They made so much noise he was convinced his parents would wake up. They stumbled around bumping into furniture and knocking over dishes. He could see their eyes scanning the room looking for something. They exchanged whispers, all of them except for her. A girl slightly older than himself was standing in the middle of the room. He could just make her out in the dark through the flickering light cast from the fireplace. He squinted trying to see her shadowy image. Her head turned in his direction and their eyes met.

Her face became lit with a brilliant light. She was beautiful. He recently turned fourteen and had begun to notice girls as different—different in a good way. But his attraction to her had nothing to do with her looks. She was calm and confident. He felt an electric charge shoot up his spine. He was totally captivated by her. She took several steps in his direction without taking her eyes off of him. The room below was now empty except for her. He knew her. He had always known her. They had just never met and he didn't know her name. The only thing that mattered to him was to her, to be with her. He floated out of the loft to the floor to stand in front of this girl. She took his hand. He did not to be asked to come with her. That went without question. ew they were going away but the reason and their destination were irrelevant. The only thing that mattered was that they would never part. Suddenly she was gone and the room was completely dark. He was cold and lonely. Santa slept on.

Mrs. Claus reentered the bed room she had shared with her husband for nearly eight decades. She looked at the tired old man dozing restlessly. He was clearly uncomfortable but there was nothing that could be done. His end was near, perhaps nearer than either of them suspected. She loved him dearly and the thought of losing him was beyond painful. Whether he would be able to hang on long enough for the spirit of Christmas to transfer to a successor was not important to her at this point. The wellbeing of her lifelong friend and partner was her only concern.

She too was tired but would not leave his side. She studied his sleeping face. It had not changed that much from when they had first met. He looked the same to her as that night in the log cabin. Marie had already seen him in her mind's eye when she found him in the book. Seeing Franz in person though left her speechless. She was not interested at all in boys until she found him. She could hardly wait to reach the cabin and she had urged the reindeer to fly faster. Adventure was impossible for Marie to resist but to actually fly was something beyond anything she could imagination. The sense of freedom was indescribable. But flying to the boy's house was more so, like the moment just before opening a gift when you are filled with wonder, excitement and anticipation. Then, upon seeing the cabin, Marie realized the experience was more than she had hoped.

In an effort to comfort him, Mrs. Claus gently held Santa's hand. His breathing eased and he immediately relaxed. Santa cracked open his eyes looking for her. He smiled contentedly.

"You're still here," he murmured.

"Of course, I am. Where else would I be?" She squeezed his hand gently and smiled.

He rested for a moment and his eyes closed. She thought he may have fallen back asleep then he looked at her again and asked, "Did Erin find him?"

"Yes."

"Well?"

"Jimmy Flipper."

Santa paused for a second then smiled again. "Little Jimmy. Of course, I should have known." He squeezed his wife's hand in return, closed his eyes again and mumbled as he drifted back to his restless sleep, "Little Jimmy...such a sweet boy."

32. The Plan

Landing in the back yard, the three friends found themselves in a similar situation as before, standing outside a building, staring intently at the windows, waiting for something to happen. Erin watched them. She followed their gaze to the house then back to her new friends. She became puzzled.

"What are you doing?" she inquired

"Shhh. We're waiting," Bort explained to her.

"Waiting for what?"

"The human," Jojo clarified.

"To do what?"

"Find us of course, what did you think?" spoke Frit.

Erin thought about this for a few seconds, as they had more experience at kidnapping people than she did, then asked, "How long do we wait?"

"Shhh!" Bort replied since watching and waiting was his area of expertise.

Erin thought about this for a few more seconds.

"What if someone else finds us?" she wanted to know.

The trio exchanged glances, quickly returning their attention back to the windows.

"It has never happened before. Only the right person can see us."

"Really?"

"We are invisible to grownups and even some children who no longer believe."

Erin coughed a brief laugh, "They can't see you?"

"No. We were surprised too, but apparently only the children who truly believe in Santa and their pets can see us."

Again Erin thought about this a bit more then asked, "So you intend to wait here until someone who can see you happens to come by?"

The three of them looked at each other and simultaneously replied, "Yes."

Erin then blurted out the obvious, "You really don't know what you're doing do you?"

They did not reply but continued with their vigil hoping for the best.

They watched in stunned silence as Erin walked up to the door and began to knock.

33. Who's there?

Jimmy was trying his best to enjoy his Tofu burger but the consistency just wasn't right. Between the tofu and soy cheese, let alone the soy milk, he thought there must be some rule of moderation that should apply. After all, human beings had been eating meat for thousands of years. He didn't actually mind the imitation ground beef but he had enough of the real thing at school to taste the difference even if the school version had suspicious ingredients. His dad meant well and was generally accommodating of Jimmy's desires but eating animals was not one of the principles his dad would compromise. Jimmy turned his half-eaten tofu burger around inspecting it.

"Speaking of learning something in school, we were reading in science about how animal protein is actually not that bad for you. In fact it has some ..."

He was interrupted by a knock on the screen door. Since it was summer the inner door was open. The screen door banged rather loudly as it bounced off the door frame with each knock. Jimmy's back was to the door and he looked up to see his father's face go pale.

Jimmy turned around and saw a young girl. She was twelve or thirteen years old he guessed, but even at that age he could see she would grow into someone very attractive. Boys' minds tend to jump to these thoughts quickly.

"What are you?" his father blurted out in a shocked tone.

"Dad!" Jimmy responded and thought to himself that his father sounded rather rude.

Being generally polite though, Jimmy pushed away from the table and walked to the door. "May we help you?" he asked through the screen. He fully expected her to say she was selling cookies or something for a fund raiser at school, but why did she come to the back door?

"We're here for you," Erin answered, then added, "to take you with us."

"Who is 'us'?" Jimmy inquired.

"The four of us, of course," replied Jojo.

A voice seemed to come from nowhere. He couldn't see Jojo or Frit. He tried to look around Erin but saw only a yard gnome on the stoop beside the girl. Gnomes are a very popular outdoor yard ornament in his neighborhood, though kind of lame in his opinion, old folk's stuff. He remembered the pranksters who stole one from the Jackson's house down the street. They drove it around the country taking pictures of the gnome at famous landmarks and mailing them to the Jackson's as if from the gnome. Some months later it returned as mysteriously as it had disappeared. Little did Jimmy, or any other human for that matter, realize was that the pictures were from the actual gnome. This was his attempt to connect with his human in a way that did not expose himself. Gnomes do, after all, need vacations too. In any case Jimmy thought seeing here was kind of weird.

"Hush," Erin said, turning her head as if someone were beside her. "Let me handle this."

Jimmy tensed a little. He looked at his dad. His father was still motionless except for his eyes that darted around seemingly at various objects.

"Dad, are you okay?" He returned his attention to Erin with a sheepish smile. "Sorry. I don't know what's wrong with him."

"It's all right," Erin replied. "Don't worry."

The longer Jimmy looked at Erin the more familiar she seemed. He shook his head slightly trying to clear it, but he found he couldn't take his eyes off of her. He hesitantly ask, "Do I know you? Are you David's little sister?"

The small voice laughed, "Of course she isn't."

Jimmy tensed, "Who said that?"

"I told you to let me handle this." Erin said, again talking to someone beside her who wasn't there. She turned back to Jimmy, "We need your help."

Jimmy was still trying to identify the source of the invisible voice. He looked at his dad. "Did you say that?" His father remained motionless. Jimmy looked back to Erin and asked, "Who said that?"

Jimmy's father finally spoke, "The elf, of course."

"The what?!" Jimmy coughed a laugh.

Jojo looked at Jimmy's father with surprise. "You can see us?"

"Of course I can. Why wouldn't I?"

"None of the other grown humans have been able to see us before," Bort responded in his deep baritone voice.

"What's going on here!?" Jimmy said in a louder voice to no one in particular.

"You are Jimmy Flipper, right?" a tiny voice from somewhere over his head asked.

Startled, Jimmy looked up and saw a large bug hovering a few inches from his face. He instinctively ducked, swatting his hand in its direction. He froze when the talking bug added, "You will come with us won't you?" It didn't sound like a question.

The deep baritone voice added, "We're here to take you to the North Pole." The yard gnome had mysteriously moved several feet closer. In addition, a tiny, thin girl with large pointed ears appeared beside Erin. It was as if Jimmy simply had refocused his eyes and there she was, like the pictures he sometimes saw that were full of random dots which could turn into an image if he crossed his eyes in just the right way. In this case, there was a girl in funny costume. Besides her pointed ears she had a pointed nose and feet and wore a red and green outfit with candy cane striped leggings. She was less than three feet tall.

The six of them looked at each other for several minutes, each surprised for very different reasons.

"What is going on here? Dad, what did you put in the burgers tonight?"

Jimmy turned back to the elf and asked cautiously, "Who are you?"

"I told you," his father repeated "She's some kind of elf."

Erin held up her hand and looked in at Jojo, Frit and Bort and declared, "Please, let me handle this."

34. Are You Nuts?

Jimmy's father invited them inside. The creatures, Erin, Jimmy and his dad sat on or around the small kitchen table covered in yellow linoleum while Erin explained the entire situation to Jimmy.

Jimmy tried to summarize. "So, let me get this straight. You guys are elves."

"I'm not." Frit replied him indignantly.

"Neither am I," Bort retorted.

"Whatever!" Jimmy continued, "You saw me in the _Naughty or Nice_ book."

"Erin did," Jojo clarified.

"You found me inside a crystal ball."

"Snow globe," Erin corrected him.

"You flew here in a miniature sleigh, with eight tiny reindeer I assume."

"No, just one," Jojo spoke up again. "We're rather small compared to the bag of toys Santa has to carry."

Jimmy rolled his eyes, "Whatever... and you intend to take me back to the North Pole to become the new Santa."

Jimmy paused, looked at his father, then at each of the four visitors. Summarizing in his most sarcastic tone, "Did I miss anything?"

The four looked at each other. Erin replied, "No, I think you pretty much covered it."

He paused, looked at each of them then burst out, "Do you think I'm stupid!?"

The four visitors and his dad jumped.

"I mean, it's one thing to pick on me at school, make fun of my name and throw toilet paper in the trees in our front yard, but you have to really think I'm an idiot to buy into this."

"They make fun of your name?" Jimmy's father asked.

Jimmy looked at his dad rolling his eyes, "Yes, Dad. They make fun of my name. They always have. They always will." He looked at Erin but was too agitated to indulge talking to the bug, the tiny doll girl or the yard ornament in front of him. "Look, Erin, you go tell your older brothers or sisters I didn't buy it and they are the dumb ones. So, go on. Get out of here!"

They all blinked their eyes in confusion and disbelief, not sure what to do next. The foursome knew they couldn't leave without him. They continued to stare at Jimmy and each other for some minutes until finally Jimmy's father cleared his throat and began speaking in a calm voice.

"You know Jimmy, this is all rather preposterous... but..." Looking at Frit he wondered, "Can you explain the talking bug?"

"You do know by now that I am actually a fairy, right?!" Frit exclaimed.

His father added, "And what about the moving yard ornament?"

"Gnome, if you please," Bort replied politely.

"The tiny girl..."

"Elf," Jojo clarified.

Jimmy's father ignored the interruptions. "The tiny girl could be wearing makeup, and if so, it you have to admit it's pretty good."

Jimmy looked at each of them for a minute then replied, almost pleading, "But Dad, this is crazy. If the other kids find out, I'm dead. I'll never hear the end of this."

Erin took Jimmy's hand and looked deeply into his eyes. "I agree this is crazy, but it is real."

He felt his heart jump at her touch. The more he looked at her the surer he was he had seen her before. He felt like he had known her all his life but didn't know where or when. "How do you know?"

"I have seen it myself. I have been to the North Pole. I have met Santa and Mrs. Claus. It's real. It's all real." She paused, she too felt her heart race slightly, then added, "I'm real too."

Jimmy's father spoke again. He suddenly like a little kid on Christmas day anxiously waiting for his parents to wake up so he could open his presents, "Can we see the reindeer?"

Without taking her eyes off of Jimmy Erin replied, "Of course, he's right outside."

As Frit led them out the back door Jimmy said out loud to himself, "This is nuts."

35. Running Out of Time

Mrs. Claus remained at the bedside of her husband constantly now. His breathing was slow and shallow. He looked at peace, as would someone who had no regrets. She knew he was not perfect. No one ever is. But he was a kind man—someone she had always loved, even before they had met.

She thought back to the time they arrived at the North Pole together. It was unlike anything she had ever seen. The houses, what few she could make out, were almost completely buried in snow even though it was still June. The roofs were simply mounds of snow. The tops of the small chimneys poked out of the otherwise barren landscape like tree stumps in a clear cut forest. White smoke lazily wove its way out of them. There were some pathways carved through the snow down to small doors leading into the houses. Inside, the rooms were lit from some unseen source. The colors of the walls and ceilings were crisp and bright like a new spring day. It felt like home, a place she would never want to leave. As it turned out, she never did, not ever regretting a minute of it.

Now she wondered how the three friends were doing along with Erin. Had they found Jimmy Flipper? Were they on their way home with him? Mrs. Claus certainly hoped so as there was very little time to waste.

36. Check It Out

The sleigh was small but just big enough to hold a couple of human passengers with a little room to spare. An elaborately decorated thing of beauty. Neither Jimmy nor his father were particularly handy around the house—they usually asked Mrs. Thompson next door to help fix things—but even they could see the high-quality craftsmanship. Jimmy smiled to himself thinking about the television commercial that talked of 'elfin magic' used to make cookies. He wondered if the same magic made the sleigh. Jimmy's father thought back to the Brothers Grimm story of the shoemaker who got help from elves to make shoes. The sleigh had velvet seats and gold trim. Jimmy wouldn't have been surprised to know the gold was real as well. It gleamed brightly in the early evening light.

The single reindeer harnessed to the front of the sleigh was the size of a large dog with antlers that were too big for his head. He nibbled the poison ivy growing out from the bottom of the fence that the lawn mower couldn't reach. He looked up as they approached nodding his head causing the reigns to shake and the bells on them to jingle. He was anxious to get back home.

Jimmy's father knelt down in front of him. They were eye to eye. As if speaking to a dog he asked, "What's your name?"

"Wah-dur," Walter replied in a garbled sort of speech.

Jimmy's father stood up quickly. He looked at Erin and Jojo. "Did he just say his name?"

Frit replied, "Isn't that what you expected?"

"Well yes, but ... I didn't think he would answer."

Frit shrugged and cast an eye roll at Bort.

Looking back at the reindeer, Jimmy's dad asked, "Your name is Wah-dur?"

The reindeer shook his head side to side, no, and returned his attention to the weeds, having lost interest in the conversation.

"His name is Walter," Jojo clarified. "Reindeer are very particular with whom they talk." Jojo scratched Walter's ear. "I'm actually surprised he bothered to answer you in the first place. He must like you."

Jimmy's dad marveled at the animal. Almost dismissively he asked, "And he can fly?"

"Of course," replied Frit. "You don't think I carried them all down here on my back do you?" and laughed in a painfully high pitched squeak. Everyone else winced at the sound. Jojo's ears folded themselves over in defense. Walter jabbed the fence with an antler.

Jojo leaned toward Erin and Jimmy and said softly, "That is the reason fairies are not allowed to help with the reindeer and why we try not to tell them jokes. It hurts too much if they find something funny which fortunately is not very often."

"What did you say?" asked Frit who overheard only bits of the exchange.

Jojo, unable to lie, simply looked at Frit, embarrassed.

Erin answered. "She was just telling us that we needed to be going."

Jimmy looked to his dad, then back to Jojo. "Wait a minute. I can't just go with you!"

"Of course you can," replied Jojo, then added insistently, "You must."

"Whoa. We just came out to see the reindeer. I never agreed to go anywhere."

Jojo, ever efficient, replied, "I'm pretty sure we covered all that inside."

Frit nodded in agreement. "After all, that's why we're here isn't it?"

"Why else?" added Bort.

"But, this is nuts. Dad, tell them this is nuts."

Jimmy's father looked at him. He then surveyed the girl, elf, fairy, gnome, sleigh and reindeer. Thought to himself then answered, "Is it, Jimmy?"

"Dad!?"

"Jimmy," his father continued, "I can't believe I am saying this, but I think they're serious."

Jimmy stared at him in disbelief.

His father continued, "If I had said this to me an hour ago I would have gone to the hospital for a head injury, but look at these... these creatures."

Bort's eyebrows furrowed slightly, and Frit glowed a little brighter at the insult.

"Jimmy, you said yourself the other day you couldn't wait to leave this town. You always talked about traveling around the country after you graduated."

"But, Dad, this isn't 'traveling around the country', this is... I can't believe I'm saying this... the North Pole, for goodness sake."

Jimmy's father's eyes lit up. "I know. Isn't it exciting?"

"But look at the reindeer, if you want to call it that." Walter's harness shook again as he raised his head to look at Jimmy. "It's too small to pull the sleigh, much less with us sitting in it." Walter pawed the ground at the suggestion.

"Oh, he's plenty big," Jojo chimed in. "These reindeer can pull ten times their own weight." Walter shook his head up and down before stretching his neck to reach a dandelion.

"I can't leave you Dad, not by yourself."

Jimmy couldn't say it, but the thought of leaving his father felt like what his mother had done to them. Utterly selfish, cruel and unfeeling. Jimmy didn't care what the reason was, he could not do that to his dad.

Jimmy's father had similar thoughts but would not stand in the way of Santa Claus. Besides, his own son leading his own life with his own adventures was the objective of most parents. Any desire to keep Jimmy close was simply unfair to Jimmy.

"Of course you can Jimmy. In fact I think you have to go."

"But, why me?" Jimmy moaned loudly.

Erin stepped forward, "I'm still asking myself the same question about me. I'm sure no one here has the answer. But what I do know, or at least what I believe, is it is not a random coincidence. There is something in you that makes you special."

Jimmy's father added, "Clearly there is something special about you, too, Erin." Erin blushed slightly and stepped back.

He then looked at Jimmy, "James Sydney Flipper, it goes without saying this doesn't happen every day. I grew up utterly in love with one person and had no desire to do anything but live out my days with her. Then the rug was pulled out from beneath me and left me with nothing... except for you. Taking care of you gave me a reason to live and I truly appreciate that, but you have a chance to do something no one else has, and you have to take it."

Jimmy's eyes looked to each of the others in turn for any support and found none. He stared at the reindeer who returned to munching on poison ivy.

"This has to be something you want to do," Jimmy's father continued. "They can't take you and I can't push you. Only you know deep in your heart, regardless of how crazy this sounds, if this is the right thing to do. Don't think about it, just follow your instincts. Is this something you feel you should do?"

Jimmy looked at Erin. She looked into his eyes, and he found the answer. Even so, he turned to his father, "I'll stay if you tell me to stay."

Jimmy's father began to cry, "I can't do that."

37. Empty Nest

Jimmy's father wiped his eyes with the heels of his hands as the sleigh lifted effortlessly into the air. He watched as it grew smaller in the dark sky. He couldn't really tell when they were totally out of sight as his eyes seemed to hold the image longer than it should. He blinked once, twice and then totally lost sight of them among the backdrop of stars. He waved knowing no one could see him do it. He stood there a few more minutes before turning and walking through the back door. The screen door banged gently on the door jamb and the back porch light flicked on. He never turned off after that night.

When anyone asked—and surprisingly few did—Jimmy's father simply told them that Jimmy had decided to go to a school out of state. There was very little fuss or concern and Jimmy gradually fell out of memory.

38. Too Late

The flight for Jimmy was just as disorienting as it had originally been for Erin. The remnants of his tofu burger began to rise in his stomach but with some effort he was able to hold it down. The flight was not a particularly comfortable but he didn't mind it so much since it gave him a chance to sit next to Erin. She seemed like a long lost friend. She felt the same about Jimmy.

Jojo was right. Walter had no difficulty pulling the sleigh. Jimmy gave up trying to rationalize how an animal could run on thin air. The sensation of flying reminded him of a recurring dream he had as a child in which he could float when holding his breath. The ground far beneath them moved past quickly. It dawned on him that in the past couple of hours everything had taken a hard turn towards the bizarre.

Jimmy's legs wobbled when they finally landed. The fantastical surroundings and colors were right out of a story book. Snow, of course, was everywhere, it was the North Pole after all, but strangely he did not feel cold. Streets were lined with candy canes, houses looked good enough to eat and strange creatures were busily moving about. A truly marvelous spectacle to behold.

"Oh my!" Jojo whispered.

Jimmy saw the worried look on her face. As far as he could tell everyone looked busy going about their business. They did not even give Jimmy a second look. But Frit and Bort also realized something was wrong. Even Erin recognized a difference from when she was here just a few short hours before.

Erin leaned over to Jimmy and said in a hushed tone, "They weren't doing this when we left."

"Doing what?" Jimmy asked, confused.

"Wandering around above ground," she answered warily.

Jimmy looked closer. Groups consisted of two or three crea-tures, each with their own kind. There were elves, of course, based on his limited knowledge of Jojo, but also what he guessed were dwarves, trolls, gnomes, fairies and ... well, other things he couldn't identify. Each of the small groups seemed to move in sep-arate directions then change their minds never seeming to actually get anywhere. The groups occasionally bumped into each other and would mumble among themselves, slightly agitated. It re-minded him of the hallways at his school between classes.

Jimmy caught a flash of movement in the corner of his eye. Bort shot into the nearest building. Frit and Jojo were close be-hind. Erin and Jimmy exchanged glances and followed. They found them in Santa's study. Jimmy saw an old woman with snow-white hair slouched in a rocking chair by the fireplace. She was surrounded by Jojo, Frit and Bort who watched her with great concern. She looked frail and exhausted. The fire was dim and the embers glowed weakly.

"Are you okay?" Frit whispered.

Mrs. Claus didn't respond but stared blankly at the fireplace. She seemed extremely detached. Erin stepped forward, past Jojo, over Bort and under Frit, and gently touched the old woman's arm. She repeated Frit's question. "Mrs. Claus, are you okay?"

She slowly raised her head to look at Erin. She smiled weakly and replied, "It's my time. That's all." Her eyes moved to the other members of the party trying to reassure them she was all right. When they fell on Jimmy she raised her hand and motioned for him to come closer. "Hello, Jimmy. It is a pleasure to meet you," she said in a soft voice.

Jojo asked hesitantly, "Where is Santa?"

Mrs. Claus remained focused on Jimmy, "Santa would have liked to have seen you one last time." She calmly leaned back in her chair and closed her eyes. "He is at peace waiting for me."

"Waiting? Waiting where?" cried Jojo.

Mrs. Claus answered quietly, "In a better place."

"Better than here?" asked Frit

"Yes. Much better than here."

Bort, unwilling to give up, asked, "What do we do now?"

"Nothing. I'm afraid it's too late."

"We failed!?" Frit concluded, terrified.

Mrs. Claus' eyes opened again and looked at Frit. "Did you do your best?"

Frit paused, then replied hesitantly, "Yes."

"Then you didn't fail.... You're just a little too late."

She settled back into her chair and relaxed again, "There was nothing more you could have done. This was just his time."

"What about the Santa Spirit?"

"I'm afraid it left with Santa."

They didn't know what to say, unsure of what to do. Was there anything to do?

Jimmy was trying to understand what was going on. Everything was happening so fast. He looked around and saw an empty chair by a large desk and sat down. He did not have the personal attachment to this place or people that the others had. He felt like a stranger at a funeral. He wanted to be polite and remorseful but at the same time had no strong feelings about any of it. He looked at Jojo sitting cross-legged on the fireplace hearth staring into the fire with Mrs. Claus. Frit was perched on a branch of the Christmas tree like a dimly lit ornament. Bort stood perfectly still at the edge of the room as he always did but didn't seem to stand quite as straight. Erin stood beside Mrs. Claus gently stroking the back of her hand trying to comfort her.

As they sat Jimmy sensed the lights dim and colors fade. There was a lot for him to digest. He found himself staring at the Christmas tree, his mind wandering back to his earliest Christmas. A vague and long lost memory seemed to emerge. He wasn't sure if real, a dream or simply an active imagination, but he recalled sitting at the top of the carpeted stairway on Christmas Eve, looking down between the banisters at the lights blinking on the tree. All the other lights in the house were off. He listened to his father snore lightly like a distant whistle. His mother was still living with them at the time. She snorted once or twice but was otherwise quiet.

He had been unable to sleep thinking of the Christmas presents beneath the tree. He thought it unfair that he had to wait until morning to see what was wrapped inside, but those were the rules. His mother never made a big deal out of Santa Claus and only offered lame attempts to pretend Santa existed. Jimmy's father played along though just in case Santa was real. He dozed with his head resting on the step above him but awoke suddenly to find a large man in red coat and pants with white trim and a white beard. He was bending down beside the tree placing something beneath it. Jimmy did not remember making any noise but the man, who could only be Santa, stood upright, turned around on his heels, and looked directly at Jimmy. Santa had sensed Jimmy's presence and precisely where he was in the room. They locked eyes. Santa looked closely at Jimmy, then smiled.

That was the end of the memory. Jimmy had always assumed it was a dream and had no recollection of what Santa might have left, or even if he mentioned it to his parents. As he grew older he convinced himself it had never actually happened. But now... now he knew that it did. Looking around this room confirmed everything he had logically ruled out as possible. He found himself angered at all the television shows and commercials that made fun of Santa with a wink and a nod, the brunt of an inside joke that simply used Santa to sell more stuff. He was disappointed by all the fake Santas who pretended to represent something they would never understand in order to make a few extra bucks. He was saddened by the kids at school who teased other kids for believing in Santa, calling them babies. He looked around the room at the piles of letters, bits of broken toys carefully stored on dusty shelves representing special memories, now lost forever. This was something so fundamentally right and good but which had become a source of ridicule and the butt of jokes. He thought of all the times he too made fun of others, laughed along with the television programs, snickered at the skinny men in oversized Santa suits and bought seasonal gadgets as gifts in a feeble attempt to show his love for his father. How did this become such a caricature of Christmas? He felt embarrassed, ashamed, sad and lonely. He felt complicit in the insincerity and selfishness of it all.

Jojo was lost in her own thoughts. She too felt somehow responsible. She knew from a practical perspective it ultimately had little to do with her, and her presence was just bad timing, but she could not stop thinking to herself why she couldn't have simply believed like all the other elves. Maybe if she hadn't been so distracted and curious none of this would have happened. What if...

Bort's mind, like most gnomes when they hide, was practically blank. This enabled him to stand for hours on end without moving. But now Bort found that now he couldn't stop thinking about the man that had saved him from certain captivity. He knew this story would rank at the top of his list and that he would never have the heart to tell it to others.

Frit already missed the human who had shown her the greatest kindness that could be expressed—helping a stranger in need. This act was unknown to her species yet here she was, unable to repay him in any way that measured up to that act of kindness he had bestowed upon her by allowing her to stay at the North Pole after being banished her from her home.

Erin looked up from Mrs. Claus who was breathing very shallow and slow breaths but whose eyes remain fixed on the fireplace's dying embers. Erin never had a chance to say goodbye to her own mother and had insulated herself from the pain she now felt. She began to quietly cry, wishing her family could come back so things could be the same as before, knowing they never would. She looked at Jimmy studying his face for the first time. They had only met a few short hours before but she felt a strange and immediate connection with him, something she had never experienced before. She didn't know if something had happened when she first saw him in the book or when she saw him in person. She just knew that they were ... connected. She felt they were made for one another in some strange way. He was looking slowly around the room at each object with great respect, curiosity and innocence. It reminded her of the time she and her family had visited a museum. Her brother had acted up but her father was mesmerized by all the artifacts studying them with humility and awe.

Jimmy's eyes made their way around the room and ended up on Erin. He too felt a connection with her. There was something about her that touched him. He looked at Mrs. Claus and his feelings of regret began to grow. If he had not resisted coming with the others maybe they would have arrived in time. He was unaware of the feelings of sadness welling up inside him or the tear gently rolling down his cheek.

39. Now What?

Jimmy absentmindedly wiped his cheek and noticed the star at the top of the Christmas tree. It pulsed slowly and ever so slightly. It seemed to brighten then fade in rhythm with his breathing. The longer he stared the brighter it seemed to become. It rose from the tree and floated towards him. He was mesmerized. Surely this was his imagination. He was afraid to look away fearing it might disappear. He felt a warmth begin to grow in his chest as it approached like the sun rising on a cool morning. It gave him a feeling of joy. The star moved closer. His sense of peace deepened. He now knew the warmth did not emanate from within himself but something that was coming to him. He didn't know how but instinctively knew this was the Santa Spirit. It reached out from the star and lightly touched his heart. It knew Jimmy for who he was. The spirit knew everything about him. It knew Jimmy's feelings, fears, dreams, wishes and aspirations. It knew everything Jimmy knew. It experienced everything Jimmy had ever experienced. Had Jimmy tried to hide anything from the spirit it would have been impossible. Then it spoke to him, not in words but with understanding.

Jimmy knew he had a choice. He could join with the spirit or remain separate. There was nothing threatening but more like coming to a fork in the road and simply deciding which path to take, except in this case Jimmy understood the implications of his choice. If he accepted he would be forever connected with the spirit. He would not be controlled by the Santa Spirit but it would be present with his every thought and act. Embracing the spirit would be a new beginning and his life would always be filled with joy. If he chose the other path this current feeling of fullness and peace would greatly diminish leaving a hole in his heart that could never be filled but he knew his life would still be forever changed.

The choice was his to make.

There would be no going back.

He thought of his father. Would his dad be okay? Then he thought of all he had learned in the past few hours and it altered his perspective on everything. He thought about the fullness he felt in the past few minutes and the sense of pure joy and contentment. Was he being selfish? "No," was the answer he heard in his head. There was much Jimmy would be able to learn and share with others and, in fact, share with the world.

He thought of the new friends he had met. He looked at each of them as he weighed his decision and saw their growing sadness. They had no idea what was happening to him. He looked at Erin. A girl he barely knew, several years younger, but something about her made him feel complete. Accepting the spirit would mean he would never be without her. Erin felt his gaze and looked back. She didn't know of the choice he was making but noticed a calm overtake him. His calm, in turn, calmed her.

In the end the decision was easy.

Jimmy did not know what to expect but knew instinctively he need only relax and give himself to the spirit. The warmth in his chest spread quickly. The lights in the room began to shine a little brighter. The smoldering fire burned a little hotter. The commotion among the creatures outside quieted. He felt fully aware. Everything glowed with an aura. Smells became pleasantly more pungent. Sounds were magnified. He felt his friends in the room and their anxieties begin to melt away. He was still Jimmy Flipper but more attuned. Any concerns he had disappeared. In an instant he was one with the Santa Spirit.

He knew everything all the previous Santas knew. Although he was just a young man he now had generations of knowledge. He realized his flaws were neither unique nor impediments. He was an imperfect human embodied by a perfect spirit.

Jimmy stood up and walked around the desk to where Mrs. Claus slumped. He felt light and his movements effortless. He knelt down and took her hand. She opened her eyes for the last time and smiled. She squeezed his hand with her remaining strength and said, "I knew you would come back."

40. Who Is That?

Jojo, Frit, Bort and Erin watched the exchange between Jimmy and Mrs. Claus with confusion. What did Mrs. Claus mean "I knew you'd come back"? Yet their feelings of fear and uncertainty lifted like a fog. They knew without being told that something special had just happened. They grew excited and glad, even as Mrs. Claus took her last breath. She relaxed her grip on Jimmy's hand and let herself pass peacefully knowing that the sprit, which had brought her so much happiness for so many years, would continue in Jimmy, and that her husband was waiting for her.

Jimmy leaned forward and gave her a gentle kiss on the cheek as one that had known her for many, many years. He held her hand until she had fully released her grip on his, then he set her hands neatly on her lap. Her head tilted forward on her chest appearing to sleep. As good an ending as anyone could wish for.

Jimmy stood up and looked at his new companions, friends he had just met but whom he knew would be his friends for life.

They were speechless trying to absorb what they witnessed.

Frit, who was standing on top of Jojo's left ear, spoke first, "What just happened?"

The ear, realizing it was a fairy's perch twitched hard, knocking Frit off balance. She tumbled off but her wings reflexively righted her in a hovering position between Jojo and Erin. Jimmy smiled.

Frit, slightly irritated by Jojo's ear, persisted, "Well?"

"I'm not really sure." Jimmy replied, then added, "But it's not like anything I could have imagined."

Erin, looking up into Jimmy's eyes, stepped toward him, reached over and took his hand. "Is what just happened what we think?"

Jimmy shrugged, paused and then with growing real- ization replied, "Yeah. I guess so." They remained silent for a few more moments, then Jimmy muttered out loud, "Dad would be totally blown away by this."

Jojo, being an elf, felt compelled to ask the obvious question, "So this means you're Santa Claus?"

Jimmy paused again, still soaking it all in, repeated again with the only words that came to his teenage mind, "Yeah. I guess so."

41. Then What?

Despite the brief period of restlessness experienced by the North Pole residents everything soon returned to normal. The elves attributed it to a bad batch of jelly beans and the gnomes thought the earthworms they ate were too old. Few if any noticed the new look of Santa as most never saw him anyway. Some of the senior elves suspected the cause but kept their thoughts to themselves.

Jimmy's transition to his new life was easier than he could have imagined. The centuries of knowledge the Santa Spirit provided allowed him to pick up exactly where the previous Santa left off. His own personality, experiences and perspectives were added to those of his predecessors, thus enriching the being he had become. Although he ultimately was a cohabitant of his body, he was fully aware of who he was as well as the ever present spirit that abided with him. A partnership in which he was more than honored to take part. Each day was filled with laughter, contentment and a remarkable sense of purpose.

Erin was not sure what her future held. She was clearly too young to become Mrs. Claus but that did not really matter to her. She did know that this was the happiest she had been since her family died and knew in her heart that her parents would approve. Jimmy became her best friend and reminded her of her brother and father. Jimmy and Erin never tired of long conversations or walks through the endless tunnels. At first the elves were disturbed when the two of them poked their heads into the work rooms or common areas but they eventually came to accept the brief distractions.

Bort and Frit remained long-term guests with Jimmy and Erin. As the snow globe had predicted, they all found each other very good companions making the transition for Jimmy and Erin that much easier. They entertained themselves with games

Jimmy never won and stories Frit never believed. But their camaraderie gave them all great joy.

Scott Schmidlick, Jimmy's original tormentor, began to mysteriously receive little gifts in his stocking when he was in high school. Scott's parents, and years later his wife, swore they knew nothing about it so he just played along. Each year he would receive a large red and white striped candy cane and a lump of black coal. Who knew Santa had a sense of humor?

Aunt Clara felt a deep guilt for Erin's disappearance even though her actions, or inactions, were unintentional. On the first Christmas after Erin's disappearance a present arrived simply signed "E". She was convinced this was a prank and the present's inexplicable appearance sealed her decision to move from the community that now ostracized her. Yet year after year the presents continued to find her, each signed in the same way. She would often think about Erin and the arrival of the mysterious present helped her believe that Erin was happy and safe. In time she began to look forward to Christmas in a way she hadn't since she was a child. She began to change and think about other people, especially neighborhood children, helping them out whenever she could. She quickly grew into a beloved member of the community.

Jimmy's father had always treasured Christmas, and infinitely more so now. His personal connection to the season was a secret he knew he couldn't share. Besides, who would believe him? Finding a gift sitting under his tree each year marked 'Santa ☺' warmed his heart immensely. He longed to see his Jimmy but he figured Jimmy was very busy and understood it was a price that had to be paid. He found some comfort in the intricately made boxes, handmade oven mitts or carefully sewn slippers that appeared each year, knowing that his Jimmy was alive and well. He proudly displayed them on his mantel, unused, as a constant reminder of his son. When friends would ask "What's Jimmy up to?" He would reply, "He's in toy distribution somewhere in Canada, but he travels a lot so I don't get to see him much anymore." They would shake their heads, disappointed in Jimmy for not being more attentive to his aging father. Jimmy's dad couldn't have been more proud.

Jojo returned to live with the other elves but not as part of the assembly line. Her calling was a Monitor elf, like Nani's had been. Jojo was widely viewed as one of the best Monitor elves ever. She showed great compassion, attention and patience with the New elves, guiding them gently and wisely. She would visit Jimmy, Erin, Bort and Frit regularly but would always return to her warren where she was prepared to answer the question, if anyone ever asked, and with absolute certainty, "Yes, humans are real."

THE END